DEDICATION

To those who desire a globally heightened level of consciousness that unites us and changes the course of our future. Light the way.

TRAPPED

THE SUSPICIOUS CASE OF ZOË SAPP

CHRISTINE RACHEAL

ISBN: 978-0-578-69019-3

Cover Illustration Copyright © 2020 by Airris Books
Cover design by Christine Racheal, Airris Books
Book design and production by Christine Racheal, www.airrisbooks.com

Cover Images by 123RF Contributors: Butus, Vitalii Krasnoselskyi, Michael Simons, Cheri Alguire, Gregory McKinney.

Although formatted and presented as journalistic interviews, *Trapped,* and each of its characters, are fictitious. Certain long-standing institutions, agencies, public offices, brands, artists and celebrities are mentioned, but the characters involved are completely imaginary. Any resemblance to persons living or dead is coincidental. However, the topics discussed within the novel are very real.

If you, or someone you know, is contemplating suicide, there is help. Call the National Suicide Prevention Lifeline at
1-800-273-8255 immediately.

OUTLINE

THE ASSIGNMENT

You can call me "Gena", but it's not my real name. Some won't bear to hear what is written in these pages, and it is best that backlash be contained to locker rooms, dinner tables, and digital rants—-all apart from me. I will say that I am a Texas-native who relocated to Atlanta after completing my Master's program.

At the time I began to write the manuscript you are now reading, I was a professional journalist with a popular publication in Atlanta. In my fourth year, our department was tasked with reporting topics that impacted the black community, so we followed each unwarranted act of violence, discrimination, and injustice. We needed to prove that the work was not finished, and urge black people everywhere to join in the fight. Aside from that, we also published articles that would help readers take preventative measures for better health and longevity, and provided economic empowerment and pointers for developing small businesses.

We created a great balance. There was

nothing outside of our scope, but we understood that topics which evoked emotion resonated most with our readers. They appreciated their voices being heard, and knew there were entities who cared enough to share the genuine, black experience with the masses. It was our duty to give them a lot of what they wanted to keep our business afloat, as well as provide open access to what they needed to help them strike a balance and push pass our issues.

The story you are about to read started in this way: Black communities began to fear that hangings were taking place in their neighborhoods. There was the high school student in Bladenboro, North Carolina; the man found hanging by a bedsheet in Port Gibson; and other documented incidents that ranged from the late 90s through 2018 when two unnamed black persons were found hanging in Atlanta, and a third was discovered in Mississippi, within weeks of each other. They were each passed off as unexpected suicides. Without a name, it would be nearly impossible to discover the truth behind these incidents. It was likely that this form of "murder" had been swept under the same rug as all the other black injustices in America, and we wanted to get to the bottom of it and find the truth.

A semi-fresh journalist hungry for a story, I searched up and down, in and out, for any leads to witnesses who could offer a juicy perspective or insight on various cases of suicide that plagued the black community. Suicide was not a "black thing" (so we believed), but somehow a November 2019 Pediatrics study showed that rates had increased amongst our youth between 1991 and 2017. If accurate, this trend would indicate that there were more young people who experienced some level of trauma, or emotional distress, or who felt hopeless or isolated. What was taking place within our community to create such a drastic rise of individuals who believed their only recourse was to end it all? Or could these numbers be attributed to foul play masked as suicide?

One evening, I randomly performed an Instagram search for the hashtag "suicide". After scrolling through hundreds of encouraging quotes, I came across the picture of a young lady who could have easily been Miss Teen USA—-a black one. She had smooth, brown skin and intense, almond-shaped eyes. Her hair was natural, curly, and she wore the style fearlessly. In the image, she simply faced the camera and smiled brightly; the girl next to her pouted her lips, tilted her head slightly, and postured herself for the perfect shot. They were so opposite that it appeared these two women were not in the same photo at all, but one had been photoshopped into a preexisting image some time later. However, they were close enough in the image to rule that out.

I read the caption, which said, "It's been almost a year. I still miss you. #ThisSucks #Suicide." The woman who created the post went by the username "Des10ee". After I determined which of the women in the picture was deceased--the beauty with the gorgeous smile--I sent "Des10ee" a message. Within an hour, she responded and shared that her best friend, a student who attended college in Tallahassee, Florida, had killed herself the previous year.

According to her, there was little to no suspicion regarding the incident, but her friend was gone, and she genuinely missed her. The story was not enough to support my research on blacks who had been found hanging from tree branches in recent years, so I thanked her for her time, called it a night, and went to bed.

The following morning, I couldn't resist the thought of the girl I had stumbled upon. I grew more curious by the hour as I wondered what led her to do it, and why she had not sought help for whatever troubled her. How could her pain and burdens be so great that her only escape was to end her life—-or had she? What darkness contradicted and overshadowed the glorious, infectious smile I saw in the image of her?

I noticed that the deceased and I had attended the same university, walked the same campus, possibly explored some of the same night life; but I was at least six years removed before she had even graduated high school. My curiosity was strengthened by the fact that I knew her name. I had an in. To this day, I cannot explain why I was lured to her story. And although it was not exactly what I was looking for, I figured it could make a great sidebar that would contribute to an even greater story.

By noon the following day, I had pitched the idea to my supervisor. Emphasizing the 73 percent increase in suicides amongst black youth in recent years sealed the deal, and I immediately received the "go ahead". I was excited to continue in hopes that I would strike gold and stumble upon the story that could mark my career in journalism, but I cannot say I was fully ready for what I discovered.

"Des10ee", whose real name is Destiny, told me that the girl in the picture was Zoë Sapp, and she was originally from Miami. I inquired about Zoë's closest living relatives, and learned that her sister, Daloris, lives in the city of Jacksonville. I was familiar. In college, I frequented Jacksonville for its access to beaches when heading west of Tallahassee proved too great an expense for the "college kid" budget. For me, this assignment would be like going home. I would be in my element, and more comfortable than if I were going some other place.

There was exactly one week between that moment and when I would be required to submit a groundbreaking article. My hope was to be recommended for a prized, journalism award, and the deadline was a mere six weeks away. I had no time to waste. Somehow, I packed my bags while simultaneously searching social media for Daloris. By the time I found her, my car was loaded with the essentials—-some business casual attire; a blue coat with large lapels that gave me Jackie Kennedy vibes when I wore it; a single pair of flats; a pair of sunglasses; my favorite shea and cocoa butter lotion; and my trusted audio recorder. I booked a hotel once I arrived in the city—-one that was budget-friendly to ensure that I could stretch my stipend and spend an entire week in the field. I landed one on the outskirts of town, and had to commute at least 20-25 minutes into the heart of the city to conduct my interviews.

After I arrived at my hotel the first evening, I developed a strategy. During my assignment, I planned to meet with several individuals who had been close to Zoë, but I had no clue who they all were yet. Regardless, I prepared a few questions for whoever was willing to share with me. Uncertain, yet determined, I would start where I stood. I was completely optimistic. My initial goal was to uncover the facts behind this young woman's premature exit from the world. Instead, I discovered how much the truth hurt each of those connected to Zoë at the time of her death.

Within these pages are their words as they were spoken to me.

INTERVIEW ONE

Date: Saturday, January 11, 2020
Time: 3:13 PM
Location: Jacksonville, Florida

SOURCE: DALORIS SAPP

Can you tell me about your sister, Zoë?

There isn't much to tell. I barely knew her.
Well, I barely knew the young adult Zoë. We
hadn't been close since she was about 11
years old.

Okay, then tell me about your upbringing.

My sister and I were both born in Kingston,
Jamaica. Before she turned 3, our parents
moved us all to the states. I was almost 9.
We landed in Swamp City--Miami. Having moved
us from the filth and violence of our
community in Kingston, my father was hopeful
that he would make even greater leaps. Our
new neighborhood was barely a notch better,
but we appreciated the subtle differences.

My father told us repeatedly that it would just be the place where we'd gain our footing before he would buy us one of those nice, two-story houses like they had in Bay Point. He said our time in our new community was like taking a flight and having a layover. We were stopping there, but it wasn't our destination. Indeed, he was a hard worker, but somehow, we knew that getting into a home like the ones in the neighborhood where my mother worked as a housekeeper and nanny, would be nearly impossible. We cheered him on anyway when he would mention it, and he smiled big at the idea.

When we first arrived in the US, he spent weekdays at the port checking the shipping containers before they were inspected by the higher-ups. On weekends, he worked in a nearby lumber yard. We had one car, so every evening we made the trek across town to pick my mother up from work. We wouldn't make it back home to eat and wash up for bed until 9 or 10 o'clock most nights, so my father would have us do homework in the car. He wasn't formally educated beyond high school, but he desired it for me and Zoë. I remember him driving and using flash cards to quiz me for weekly spelling tests.

What were your earliest memories of Zoë?

Zoë's birth was like showing up for a job I never formally accepted. From that day, my home life consisted of getting bottles, changing her, sharing food, being forced to share and play nice. My earliest memories are of trying to accept that the easy life I'd had before Zoë was born, was completely gone. It was unnatural.

~

One Saturday, while our father was away at work, our mom took us to play at a small park a few blocks from our apartment. It was the only one in the neighborhood, and it always had more children who wanted to play than equipment. Some kids would wait patiently for their turn; others would just pile onto the sliding board or swing set and eventually drive the others away; or the bad asses would come into the park and demand whatever they wanted. If your mama wasn't there, they typically got it.

It was hot outdoors, but the wind would sweep through and cool us off on occasion. My mother sat on a bench near the chain-linked gate at the park's entry, and watched as we played. I didn't notice any other parents in the park that day, but I knew that at least Zoë and I were safe from little tyrants who wanted their way. My mother was very stoic in posture, and she would only move from her position if we were preparing to leave.

Like most days, the playground overflowed with neighborhood kids who tried to busy themselves on a school-less Saturday. I patiently pushed a girl my age on the swing with hopes that she would soon get off to give me a turn, and possibly return the favor. The sun was relentless, and I could feel myself baking as I pushed and pressed the girl higher into the pleasant breeze. I realized it could be a while before she desired to trade places, so I walked away for her to continue in ecstasy without my help.

At the time, Zoë was four, and capable of handling most of the equipment in the park. A set of dome-shaped monkey bars on the far end of the park had the least amount of attention, and that's where Zoë had successfully climbed up the first two levels. The slide had a line of kids waiting to come down, and other hardheads who attempted crawl up from the bottom. I decided to retreat to where my mother was sitting and wait them out in the shade. Thirst or their burning skin was sure to drive them away at some point.

As I took a seat beside my mother, Zoë had reached the top of the monkey bars. And no sooner than she'd done it, she tumbled down, and hit her head on one of the metal bars in the process. I saw the entire incident, but my mother didn't tune in to what had happened until Zoë was already crying on the ground beneath the monkey bars.

"Oh no, God!" she said as she ran over to Zoë.

I didn't move from my position, but I could see what transpired very clearly. Zoë screamed as my mother picked her up. I thought my sister would wrap her arms around her and wail until the pain had passed, but she didn't. Zoë looked over to me as my mother tried to comfort her. Her arms were extended towards me as though she wanted me to pick her up. I heard her cry, "D! Please!" I didn't move.

Zoë climbed down from my mother's grip and wept as she walked over to me—arms still extended in front of her. She slowed her pace as she came closer to me, and she used one of her hands to wipe tears from her face. Dirt from her hand mixed with her tears, and the mud was smeared over her eyes. Grains of sand must have gotten in because she shrieked immediately. "D! Please!" she cried.

I grabbed her hands and dusted them off with my shirt, and then used the other side of my shirt to wipe her face. She desperately wanted to escape her discomfort, so she blinked her eyes as quickly as she could to sweep away the particles. I lifted each eyelid and blew into them with all my might. Whatever I couldn't do, I believe her tears did the rest.

I finally noticed her knee. "You're bleeding, Zoë," I told her.

My mother stood next to us, and didn't say anything. She watched me play nurse to her baby, and I can't say it was easy for her. Her arms were open and she was ready to move when needed. I could tell she wanted to hold Zoë but probably feared being rejected by the screaming girl again.

"I don't have anything for your leg," I shrugged.

My mother reached down next to where she sat on the bench and handed me a wide, plastic cup of ice water she had brought from home. "Pour," she said.

Zoë's hands pressed into my lap. As the cold water ran down and saturated her socks, she was soothed to just a whimper. When she saw that the blood had been washed away, she climbed onto the bench next to me and examined the damage. It wasn't much—just a scrape on her knee that was deeper in some areas than others, but the bleeding had stopped without any pressure. Zoë rested her head on my shoulder as she tried to steady her breathing after crying. Her snot oozed onto my shirt, which was soiled by the dirt from her face. I was beyond ready to go home. My mother must have agreed because she grabbed her bag, and the cup, and we walked back to our apartment—Zoë's hand holding tightly to mine.

~

How would you describe your mother?

She was a quiet woman, but she was forced to

be that way. She never protested or rejected anything my father would say or do. She was always agreeable, but I'm sure outsiders saw her as a pushover. They didn't know what happened in our home.

Can you tell me what was happening there?

I was 4 when I saw my mother's bloody nose for the first time, and 7 when I first sat next to her hospital bed. Over time, she had become so accustomed to my father's beatings that she gathered enough bandages, gauze, ointments, and medications for her own recovery kit. Unless she broke a bone, she would just fix herself up at home.

I don't recall a time she ever raised her voice at him. Unless there was some secret affair, or something else I was unaware of that caused his anger, she didn't do anything to provoke it. When it came to her children, he wouldn't let her verbally correct us or discipline us for poor behavior. It got to the point that she stopped speaking to us altogether. She would cook our food and prep our clothes for the week, but my father ordered us to the dinner table, or to the bathtub, or to get our books to head to school. She would kiss on the forehead, and we could feel her breath on our faces, but that was the fullness of her interaction with us.

Were you and Zoë also abused by your father?

He wasn't abusive towards us—-just her. Although he would say it, it was hard to believe that he loved my mother. On the other hand, she would do anything for him, and she proved it until the day she died. Zoë and I were both there.

Can you take me back to that day?

Unfortunately, I can.

~

It was the winter of 2003. Port workers were being laid off left and right, and my father was amongst them. Not only had he not fulfilled his mini-mansion promises, he had been out of work for almost three months and, no matter how much he begged, the lumber yard wasn't able to give him additional shifts.

My father had always been a heavy drinker, so nothing was new except the increased amount of time he had to do it. When we arrived home from school, the stench of his daily ganja sessions would be in the air, and we would find him sprawled across the couch in the living room. When it was time, we would wake him for the drunken adventure across town to pick up my mother because, even though he didn't need it, he wouldn't allow her to take the car.

Me and Zoë, who was in an early education program at my school, came home one day and found my father in a way that was typical for him—lying across the couch. The furnishings in our apartment were minimal, so his presence took up a lot of space. Our apartment was small. There were only two bedrooms, and a living room no larger than one of the bedrooms. So, there was only a small sofa, a chair that didn't match anything else in the room, a coffee table, and an old, dusty rug my father found near a dumpster when we'd first moved there.

I passed my father on the way to our bedroom. Sweat beaded on his forehead, and he muttered something in patois that I couldn't quite make out. When I returned, I opened my activity book on the coffee table in front of him and kneeled to complete my assignment.

"Can I eat?" Zoë walked into the room and asked innocently.

"Give me a minute. I gotta finish this before we get Ma," I told her.

"But I'm hungry, D," she begged.

I looked at my father, who began to turn over on the couch. He was always a clean-shaven man, but his dreadlocks were long enough to swipe his butt when he walked. As he laid there, a few of his locs wrapped around his body and were being tugged at the scalp, and I knew he would soon awake. I didn't want Zoë's whining to disturb him, so I jumped up and went into the kitchen.

I checked the fridge for leftovers, but the containers had been emptied and placed in the sink, which was overflowing. To compensate for the filth in our community, my mother worked hard to keep a clean house. I would hear her scrubbing floors and cleaning dishes throughout the night, and I would awake to the smell of that day's dinner before she got herself ready for work. Yet, there wasn't anything there. I checked the freezer, and there was a single bag of frozen fish. I didn't know how to prepare it.

"There is nothing here," I said to Zoë, and she lowered her head disappointedly.

I reached for a cup from the cabinet and filled it with the last few ounces of punch left in the container. "Here. Drink this."

I knew it wouldn't satisfy her hunger, but it would keep her quiet. She went back into our bedroom to continue building a fort out of pillows and blankets. I returned to my position near my father and got back to my studies.

It was almost 6 o'clock, and time for us to pick my mother up from work.

"Daddy." I nudged him. "Daddy, wake up."

"Yuh wan guhl? Mi restin'." He rolled over again.

He seldom used patois when he spoke to us. When he did, it was blended with standard English. We would hear him speak with others from our native land, fully in patois, and their speech seemed to connect them.

"It's 6, Daddy." There was silence initially, and then he opened his eyes wide and sat up on the sofa.

"I'm up. Where yuh sister?"

"Zoë!" I called, and when she appeared, my father smiled—big. She ran into his lap and nearly stepped on me in the process.

"Der mi guhl," he paused, and looked at me. "Yah bote mi guhls." He caressed my chin to make me feel included.

He used his hands to beat rhythmically on his lap, and then shifted a few *pats* to Zoë's. It went on for a minute, and she laughed and moved her head to the beat.

"'Member dem drums? Ah." He smiled and continued the sound. "Yuh know." She giggled some more.

My father had grown up Nyabinghi—the Rastafarian group known for their drumming worship—but he had long abandoned the practice for reasons unknown. In the States, our religious practices were a mixture of Nyabinghi, Pentecostalism, and whatever Daddy said.

"Let's go," he ordered. When he stood, he blinked slowly and stopped a moment before he took his first step. "Come on. Come on."

Obedient, we followed him. When we hit the front door, the cold air whipped our faces and we realized that our jackets were still inside. Daddy wasn't one who liked being turned around, so we kept moving—arms wrapped tightly across our chests and shivering. The car was a great refuge from the cold.

During the ride, I could hear Zoë's growling stomach, but it went unnoticed by my father.

"Just wait," I whispered to her.

When my mother got into the car, a bit of chill entered with her, and the car's heat completely escaped. We trembled.

"Where yah jackets? You know betta dan dis," she said.

"No point correctin' dem now," my father responded. "Dem fine."

"I don't wan dem sick."

"I say, 'dem fine'," he raised his voice and my mother immediately backed down.

When we pulled into the complex, my father dropped us off, and we went inside where it was warm. He didn't say where he was going, only that he would be right back.

My mother removed her shoes in her bedroom, and slipped into her favorite housedress—blue with white clouds printed all over. And then she went into the kitchen to see the wreckage. There was nothing left of her prepared dishes, so she removed the frozen fish from the freezer, and a bag of rice from the cabinet.

"Yah eat *any* ting?" she asked me, and I shook my head.

She added water to a small cooking pot, along with a portion of rice, and placed it on the stove before putting the fish into a bowl of water to thaw it quickly. She turned her attention to the dishes, and began to wash them when my father returned. He stumbled a little, and his shoulder collided with the edge of the kitchen wall as he approached us.

"Cookin', eh?" He smiled. "I see. I see."

He staggered into the bedroom and stayed there for a few minutes. I sat at the kitchen table—worn wood, round, and it wobbled at the slightest touch. There were only three chairs, so we never ate there together, but it was where I could watch my mother. She didn't speak much, but she didn't have to. I learned by watching. I observed her care for the cleanliness of each dish, the patience with which she would peel and chop fruits and vegetables, the sound of her voice as she hummed. She was a graceful woman.

After a while, my father reemerged from the bedroom and joined her at the sink. He grabbed her waist and slobbered on her neck.

"Wait," she said. "Let me feed dem."

"Can't." He continued to kiss on her neck.

She saw me from the corner of her eye. "De chile."

He turned and faced me, placing his weight against the counter. My father's eyes were different. We were used to them being veiny and red, but that night they were animalistic, wide, and scary.

"You wan go to bed?"

I shook my head to reject the idea.

"Mommy does," he said, and moved quickly to grab her by the waist. She could barely turn off the running faucet before he whisked her into the bedroom and slammed the door. I could hear a bit of commotion at first. My mother said something in objection, and then there was a hard thud against the wall. I sat and listened, and watched the trembling, covered pot of rice that boiled rapidly on the stove. I heard my father panting, and a few squeals from my mother, but their sounds did not frighten me.

Zoë walked into the kitchen and interrupted my observation.

"D, I'm hungry," she said.

The thick rice water bubbled out and sizzled against the eye of the stove.

"Can we eat?" she asked.

"Not now. It's not ready."

"When then?"

"I don't know."

A bit of smoke began to rise from beneath the pot of rice. I walked over to turn it off, but I was too afraid to reach behind the violently boiling pot to shift the knob.

Zoë joined me at the stove. "Can we eat it, D?" she asked.

I was annoyed. She didn't have the maturity to measure the intensity of the moment.

"Move." I shoved past her and went over to my parents' bedroom door. I knocked—quietly at first, but when it went unacknowledged, I knocked a little harder.

"What yah wan, guhl?" I heard my father say.

"Daddy." I hesitated. "Zoë's hungry. The stove is smoking."

My mother quickly emerged from the room, stretching her housedress towards her knees. She removed the lid from the rice pot and the water dwindled out of view. She grabbed a knife from the drawer, and started to cut at the partially frozen fish.

My father came after her, glistening and wild-eyed.

"Get back in der," he commanded.

"Let me get dem food, Charles." She went to move the fish from one side of the counter to the other to get away from him and, for a moment, she and I locked eyes for the last time. Her eyes were different too. They weren't red, but they were larger than normal and possessed by a fear that she couldn't articulate.

"Get back in der," he yelled and pointed towards the bedroom door.

She dropped the knife into the fish water, and turned to face him. "Please." She held her hands out in front of herself and he slapped them away. In the same swift movement, he wrapped a single hand tightly around her throat. She squealed, choked, and then gasped for air. They tussled as my mother attempted to fight back.

"Stop it!" Zoë cried.

I couldn't muster any tears because I knew she needed help. I reached backwards for the wooden bird sculpture my mother kept in the center of the kitchen table. I gripped its head, which was narrow enough for my hands to wrap around, and I raised the solid base into the air and charged at my father. I whacked his flesh as hard as I could, and my strike collided painfully with his shoulder blade. He released my mother and grabbed at his back.

"Yuh wan do dat ting?" he panted and blinked his eyes as if he could barely see. "To me?" He couldn't keep his balance. He staggered into the counter as he reached for the throbbing pain in his back. And then his eyes rolled upwards. He closed them for a second, but when they reopened, it was as if his high had been elevated and he was riding an unexpected, turbulent wave. He looked at his hands; he looked toward us, and then to my mother who held tightly to the counter to catch her breath. He reached for his back again.

"Oww," he said painfully. "Yah a mad one, guhl."

He turned towards the counter. I couldn't see where his hand was going, but when he turned around again, he had buried the handle of the fish water knife in his fist, leaving the blade completely exposed and dripping behind the pinky finger of his right hand.

"Yah gawn mad, chile? Yah tink yah are?"

I shook my head and began to cry. I wasn't afraid; I hoped my tears, coupled with Zoë's, would cause him to finally stop.

My father pushed off from the counter, and I assumed he was coming towards me, but my mother stood swiftly and yelled, "No!" It must have caught him off guard because he impulsively thrusted his right hand in her direction. We watched. My father's hand no longer held the knife. It was lodged firmly into the center of my mother's chest. She fell to the floor. My father's mouth gaped open, and he looked at his hands, and then at us, and then at our mother.

Zoë's wails couldn't be ignored as she watched our mother gasping for air.

"No, no. Come." He ran over and picked Zoë up to carry her outside, and away from the scene.

I kneeled next to my mother who wouldn't look at me; she stared in shock at the knife protruding from her chest as blood saturated her favorite housedress. As badly as I wanted to, I didn't know how to help her. She gurgled for a while before my father came back, and then she was quiet. Her eyes, open.

"Lilly," he called when he walked in, and I moved quickly to the farthest corner of the room.

He wept, knowing she was no longer there.

"I didn't mean dat." He sat on the floor next to her, and cradled her in his arms. "I didn't mean dat."

That night, my father was an animal. He wasn't his normal self—nor his sober self, or his high-off-his-ass self. Something more badass than alcohol and ganja had consumed him. Whatever it was, I never saw. I would say he spared me from witnessing his drug use the same way he spared Zoë from our mother's final moments; but I would see a lot of drug use where Zoë and I were headed.

My mother had a cousin who had lived in Miami for about ten years before we came. We called her "Juby." The night my father was locked up, he told police he wanted us to stay with her. He insisted that his kids not enter the system. To this day, I don't understand how Juby's place was any better.

We moved into a rundown, three-bedroom home a block from the Pork N Beans projects. There was never any hot water, lukewarm at best, and we were always outnumbered by cockroaches and mosquitoes. Juby had three children: Lena, Andre, and Jevaun. They all lived in the home with her, along with random strangers who would come over to party with Juby for a few days, crash on her raggedy couch, and then disappear for another junkie to have the space. When we were at Juby's, we kept ourselves locked in the room to avoid butting heads with her "guests"; and when we were away from Juby's, our absence went unnoticed. There wasn't a curfew or set rules. The only thing Juby would say is, "Don't get caught," and would send us on our way.

She was on government assistance, had food benefits, and her rent was cheaper than a storage unit, so we survived. And that was better than being dead or in prison like our mother and father.

~

What was Zoë like after your mother was killed?

At first, she didn't understand the concept of death. No one was there to plan for my mother's funeral, so the county cremated her. Zoë didn't see her condition when she died to know how finite it was. She thought everything was temporary, and that our parents would come for us. She missed our father most; she asked for him almost every day for over a month.

Emotionally, Zoë was as she had always been. She clung to me, but that wasn't new. I don't remember her ever crying about our parents not being around. If anything, she cried most about the conditions their absence had left us in.

Was it better to have Zoë with you at Juby's place instead of being separated by the state?

No. Juby's place wasn't suitable for kids Zoë's age. Shit, Juby's place wasn't suitable for *anybody*. I thought my responsibility for Zoë was tough before our parents were gone, but it was worse at Juby's. I had to make sure she ate, bathed, had decent clothes to wear, and that Juby's crackhead friends wouldn't mess with her. There were many times that I wanted to ignore her and leave her to defend herself, but I couldn't do it. I saw

my mother when I looked at Zoë, and it forced
me to do the best I could by her.

~

Every day, I walked Zoë to school. Her start time was about
an hour before mine, and if I didn't see to it that she was there on
time, no one else would. I dropped her off in the cafeteria when
there were only a few workers preparing breakfast for the students'
arrival. I'm sure it was quiet and lonely for Zoë, but she was there,
and she was safe. I was usually late to my first period class because I
couldn't ride the bus from our neighborhood like the other kids.
After I left Zoë, I had to walk a half hour to the middle school.
Excessive tardiness didn't bother me. My teachers were made aware
of the situation Zoë and I faced at home—and not because I told
them. My English teacher called to complain about my tardiness to
Juby one afternoon. In response, she received a firm "those ain't my
damn kids" from the woman who was listed as our guardian.
Everything was self-explanatory from that point forth.

Staying in school wasn't easy. Our entire community was
poor, but many of the people worked and at least *tried* to care for
their families. Juby didn't. Whatever food there was in the house, we
went out ourselves to get it. If our clothes were clean, it's because
we washed them in the kitchen sink, or bathtub, with dish-washing
liquid. As Zoë grew out of her clothes, I would give her the ones I
had also grown out of, but they would still be too big for her frame.
None of that mattered if we could go to school and not have to put
up with Juby. While most children look forward to it, summers were
the worst for us.

When Zoë was seven, she came home from school
complaining of a stomach ache. I was in the middle of braiding a
girl's hair to make a quick $20, so I told her to go and lie down. She
listened, but I noticed she would get up and go into the bathroom
every half hour or so. By the time I finished the girl's hair, Juby's
entourage of dope-heads had gathered on the front porch, and the
sun had already set. I went into the bedroom I shared with my sister
and Lena, Juby's daughter. Zoë was balled tightly into fetal position
on the bed. She was sweating profusely, and the tiny droplets ran
down forehead. Her eyes were heavy, but she was fully awake.

"You alright?" I asked.

"No. It still hurts," Zoë said.

"Your stomach?"

"Yes."

"What you doing in the bathroom?"

"I had to throw up."

"A lot?"

She nodded her head, and I touched her face with the backside of my hand. She was burning up. I had never seen Zoë sick before. She was always a healthy girl, and seldom needed a doctor's office visit, but that evening she should have been quickly swept away to the emergency room.

I went to the front porch where Juby, dressed in a raggedy housecoat and barefoot, sat on the stoop and drank with three of her friends—an older woman with jagged teeth, and two men who could both use a hearty meal to cover their bones.

"Juby," I said.

"What you want, chile?" She took a swig of her drink.

"Zoë's sick. She said her stomach hurts, and she's hot."

"That ain't nothin'. What you want me to do?"

Taking Zoë anywhere was obviously out of the question in Juby's condition, so I didn't mention the thought. "You have any medicine?"

She laughed. "I look like I take medicine?" She held up a near-empty bottle of rum. "This all the medicine I need—and some other shit I ain't gon' mention." Her comrades laughed.

"What about the medicine cabinet? Can I look?"

Juby's countenance became serious. "What the fuck I just said, girl? I ain't got none." She held up the bottle again and examined it as she swished the contents around. "I know. Bring her here. I got something for her."

I didn't move. I could sense that Juby's plan wasn't conventional, so I just stared at her.

"You heard what I said. Tell her, 'come here'."

I backed away and went into the house. Zoë was still balled up on the bed, eyes closed, but not asleep. I nudged her.

"Juby said to come to her."

Zoë seemed dizzy, and her movements were slow. Her eyes moved at the pace of a snail. I helped her to stand, and we walked out of the room together; her shirt was damp with sweat.

When Juby saw her in the doorway, she stood and came closer to us.

"You sick?" she asked.

Zoë barely had the strength to nod. She put her hands against her belly and mumbled, "My stomach hurts."

"You ain't pregnant, is you?"

Zoë shook her head and slowly closed her eyes. She was

14

incredibly weak.

"Good. Then you can have some of this." She screwed the top from the bottle of rum and threw it to the ground. "Open your mouth. This will help you feel better."

Zoë couldn't resist the alcohol being poured down her throat. The bitterness and burning sensation of liquor caused her to gag and spit it out. Juby's immediate response was to shove her, and Zoë collided with the doorframe.

"This good liquor. You wastin' my shit," Juby said as she pointed a finger within an inch of Zoë's face. "Don't do it again, or I will kick your ass. Drink it."

Juby shoved the glass bottle back into my sister's mouth, which clanked against her front teeth. Zoë swallowed the remnants of the bottle as liquor dripped down both sides of her chin.

"Now take your ass in there and lay down." Juby returned to her guests.

I walked with Zoë back into the bedroom and she sat haggardly on the bed. I assumed she would immediately crawl back into fetal position, but she didn't.

"Lay down so you can feel better," I told her.

"No." She pressed a hand against her chest. "It hurts."

"It'll go away. Just lay down."

After a moment, Zoë fell onto the floor from the bed. She dry-heaved violently. I grabbed a dirty t-shirt and kneeled next to her.

"Throw up on this," I said.

She continued to dry heave, and then stopped. Her eyes were closed softly as though she had finally found a moment of rest. I thought Juby's plan had worked until Zoë suddenly vomited into the shirt in my hand. Her body wanted to produce more than what her stomach contained, and she was in pain. I couldn't decipher her tears from her sweat as she rolled on the floor.

I went into the kitchen for a glass of water, passing a drunken Juby in the hall along the way, and returned to Zoë as quickly as I could.

"Try to drink this," I said.

She lifted her head and took in a single gulp.

She placed her cheek against the floor and extended her arms in a way that made a "W" shape with her body. She dug her nails into the carpet and began to dry heave again. "D, I don't feel good," she said, facing away from me.

"I know, Zoë. I know."

I watched her tremble and heard her moans, but there was

nothing more that I could do, and she knew it. Zoë laid in that condition for another hour until she fell asleep on the floor. By morning, she could move around a little, but was without an appetite.

~

For how long did you and Zoë live with Juby?

A little over five years. School was almost out for summer, and Juby got a chance to move to New York with some relatives who had gotten settled there. We didn't know Juby had moved for three days after she left. The boys were gone, but Lena was still around. She was almost 18. I guess Juby couldn't even take all her own children.

On the third day, I went home from school and a CPS worker stood at the chain-linked gate in front of Juby's house. When I approached, he asked my name and wanted to know my sister's whereabouts. When I told him she was still in school, he made a phone call to have her picked up, and told me to get into his car.

I didn't see Zoë. That evening, I was placed in a foster home close to the beach. There were two other kids there, but I didn't attempt to get close to anyone. I knew my stay wouldn't be long. I was on track to graduate, and I would soon turn 18.

Zoë was 11 at the time, so her experience in foster care would be different from mine. She would have at least another seven years of living with random families——and without me.

Did you try to find her?

The people at Child Protective Services told my foster parents where she was, but I didn't visit her.

Why not?

For the first time, I didn't have to think about Zoë. And while it's not easy to say how good it felt, it did. I finished high school, worked odd jobs around the city and rented a room in the back of an old couple's house, and then I met a man who was a few years older than me. He was in the Navy, and wanted to commit faster than I had time to think. So, I was married at 19. I won't lie and say I thought of Zoë often. I didn't.

Do you believe you loved your sister?

I had my moments. I did. But there were many days in childhood that I couldn't bear the sight of her. She was the protected one--if not by my parents, by me. What I constantly play back about the night my mother died is not the blood-stained dress or the knife sticking out of her chest. I think back to the moment I let Zoë annoy me into intruding upon whatever was happening in that bedroom. When I consider how things could have been different, and my mother still here, I think of that--not the knife in my father's hand, or the sculpture that pounded his back.

That's a lot to admit, Daloris.

I know, but I might as well tell the truth. When Juby abandoned us in Miami, I knew that

I was both book smart and street smart, and I could figure it out. I also knew my sister was fragile, and a part of me wanted her to suffer through the foster care system. Don't judge me, please.

I thought Zoë was prettier than I was. She took after our mother; her skin was brighter, and she had eyes that demanded attention. She was pretty without a speck of makeup, and with hair that hadn't been washed or styled for weeks. She didn't need any of those things. But her teeth--I'm sorry, I can't help but laugh--her teeth were the worst I had ever seen. They were extremely crooked, and more crowded than a bar in a college town. Two of her bottom teeth were rotting because she refused to brush them when I told her, and she had two teeth that grew behind the others. People complimented her looks when we were kids, and would say how cute she was; but I secretly waited for Zoë to laugh, or speak with her mouth open wide enough, to diminish their praise for her.

I last saw her ten years ago—-2010. I travelled to Miami and, to my disappointment, she was in the same foster home that had taken her in two years before, and she was happy. She was at the height of puberty, so she sported a few pimples along with a shiny set of braces.

She showed me the flute she played in her middle school band while we were in her bedroom—-a space she didn't have to share with anyone.

I can't explain it, but a part of me broke to see her living so well. I stayed for about a half hour before I lied and told her I risked missing the bus back to Jacksonville if I didn't leave in time.

I could tell it was hard for Zoë to see me go, but it would be harder on *me* if I stayed.

Did you connect with her at all after that visit?

Yes. She would call or text me every other week, and tried to find any reason for a visit, but I always brushed her off. I just couldn't do it.

Is it that you couldn't stand to see her doing so well, or did her presence remind you of the hardships of your past?

Both. I was convinced that my separation from Zoë could help redeem the years I was consistently there for her--years when no one was there for me. I wanted Zoë to feel as alone as I felt all that time. It was unfair. I got so carried away with being bitter--believing she deserved my abandonment--that even into adulthood, I kept my distance from her. I settled on the idea that she didn't need me anymore anyway.

Is it possible that you wanted Zoë to need you?

No. Wait. I don't know. I wanted the life that was stolen from me because of her. I've seen television shows where people are shown what life would be like for others if they had never been born. And I thought about it myself a few times. What if Zoë had never been born? How much better could my life have been?

You don't believe your father would have eventually killed your mother?

I know that Zoë wouldn't have urged me to go into the room and upset my father the night he killed her. That's enough to believe that my life could have been different—-better—-without her.

I guess that explains how you were only two hours away from Zoë once she went off to college, and you still never saw her.

I didn't say I was proud of my strained relationship with Zoë. There are things I still don't understand about why I felt what I did for her, so I don't expect you to understand by the end of this little interview. After we separated at Juby's, I was entitled to all the choices I made. I chose to not have a relationship with her. And over time I no longer knew Zoë. We talked on occasion, but I can't say I knew her.

I can respect your honesty. Who would you say knew her best?

I don't know. Probably the foster mother she had, Gayle. They seemed to get along pretty good when I was there. She didn't call the lady "mama", but you could tell Zoë was doing more than just crashing there. They cared for each other.

If you don't mind, I want to shift gears. Talk about the most memorable experience

you shared with your sister.

I won't say it's a *good* memory, but after my mother's death, there is one other experience I will never forget.

~

It was a Monday. Zoë was eight. Everyone in Juby's home had a way to make money, legal or illegal, except Zoë. I remember trying to start this hustle where we would take our old coloring books, rip out the used pages, and try to sell them on the block, or we would go to the dollar store and buy a few coloring books and crayons to sell for double or triple the cost. People knew what we were up to, but when they saw Zoë's big, bright, begging eyes, they bought them. We couldn't get to the store often because stores with good books weren't in our neighborhood. We would have to wait for Juby to go across town before we would beg her to make a stop for some books. So, Zoë had the least access to cash.

Juby's 10-year-old son, Jevaun, was a lookout for the local riff raff who would break into people's cars or homes and steal from them. They would give him $5 - $10 each time he went with them to keep watch. He usually saved it until he had enough to buy some new kicks. He had just bought a new pair before his last hit. So, the pot, wherever he stashed it, was near empty when it went missing. He said that when he hid it away, Zoë had just returned home from school and walked in on him as he pushed the small pickle jar of cash deep into his laundry bin. The money was there the day before and, according to him, only Zoë had seen where it was hidden.

When Zoë came home from school that day, she rushed past everyone and went straight into our bedroom. Juby was beyond furious. When her son explained what had happened, I heard numerous "lil bitches" being yelled from the back room where she slept. She didn't speak to me about it, but waited to confront my sister in the living room. They called her back.

"Get in here, girl," Juby yelled as she rested her arm on a couch pillow. Smoke rose from the burning cigarette in her hand. Ashes fell to the pillow.

"My mama want you, Zoë!" Jevaun called out.

"Ma'am?" Zoë returned.

"Jevaun said you took something that belongs to him."

Zoë looked at me as if I could answer for her.

"Did you?" Juby asked. Zoë didn't say anything; she just

hung her head. "I'll take that as a *yes*. Stealing will get both of your little asses tossed out of here," Juby said as she directed her speech at me. She looked back to Zoë. "But I'm gonna kick your ass good for stealing from my boy." She pulled on her cigarette.

I'd seen Juby beat her kids before, and it was far from easy to watch. She sent her oldest son, Andre, to the hospital for stitches after slicing his right brow open with a wire clothes hanger—her object of choice. As angry as I was for the position my sister had put us in, I didn't want that for her.

"I'll do it," I said.

"What?" Juby asked.

"My mama didn't raise no thieves. I wanna whoop her ass myself." I conjured a bit of steam as I *huffed* to make my anger believable.

"Alright then." Juby sat back in her chair and smoke billowed from her lips. "Get to it then. And you better not hold back," she said. "I don't give a fuck if it's a dime or five hundred dollars, stealing in this house is asking for an ass whooping. Go on now."

"Come on." I grabbed Zoë's shirt by the collar and accidentally scratched her chin with my nails, but I didn't acknowledge it. I yanked her towards the bedroom. I believe she initially thought I wouldn't do it—that I would just turn out the lights and pretend nothing happened. I couldn't do that, but what I would do to Zoë would not be worse than what Juby would do.

I went to the closet in search of a belt—one possibly left behind by one of the men Juby or Lena entertained—one that was thin enough to get a good grip, but thick enough for her to feel it. I found what I was looking for in a black garbage bag of old clothes stuffed in the back of the closet. When I turned and she saw it dangling from my hand, Zoë immediately burst into tears.

"Take off your pants," I commanded.

She wept as she removed a shoe; its worn, rubber lip flapped as it fell to the floor. She removed the other shoe, and one of her toes stuck through her pink sock. I wanted to laugh, but I caught myself.

"Hurry up. I don't have all day."

She pulled down her pants, and stomped them to the floor. "But please," she begged as snot gathered along her top lip. "I'm sorry, D. I won't do it again. Please."

"Turn around," was my final order.

I had never given that kind of beating to anyone before, but I knew to aim for her butt and the meaty parts of her thighs where the sting would be great. My method was to count the purple polka dots on her panties, draw back, and then pop her again before counting the next dot. There had to be at least twenty, but I stopped counting when I became dizzy from exhausting all my energy and nearly overheating. I was tormented by the lack of circulating air in the bedroom, but I could hear the door rattle and see shadows of feet as they walked near the door, and I knew I couldn't stop. I'm sure I hit her more than the purple dots I counted, but she didn't stop pleading—even when it was clear that her punishment was inevitable and already in motion. Thinking back on it, I couldn't have been hitting her *that* hard—I wasn't too swift or strong. I think the emotional pain that stemmed from my commitment to carry out her punishment outweighed the whooping she received.

Suddenly, the buckle swung loose from my sweaty grip and the final lash drew blood. The thin prong sliced deeply across the back of her right thigh, and she screamed. I dropped the other end of the belt as she fell to her knees. She attempted to touch her wound, but the sting would drive her hand away.

How could I help the person I also caused to suffer? So, "Put your pants back on, Zoë," was all I could think to say.

She did as she was told, irritating her newly-formed welts every inch of the way. My job was done. I walked out of the room and basked in the cooler air outside before I went into the kitchen to cook that evening's meal.

Zoë didn't speak for the rest of the evening. She sat alone on the back porch while each of us grabbed a plate of rice, beans, a few plantains, and stuffed our faces. When it was time for bed, she changed her clothes in the bathroom, and then fell asleep in a living room chair.

After my shower, when everyone was asleep, I went into the room I shared with the other girls, got into bed, and immediately noticed that something had been stuffed inside my pillow case. I reached in, and pulled out a white box large enough to cram in a fist.

I opened it. It was a strawberry cupcake—my favorite treat at the time—from the bakery near Zoë's school. Written inside the lid was, "Happy birthday to my sister, D. I love you," and I remembered I would turn fifteen the following day.

Zoë understood what it was like to have one birthday after another go unacknowledged, and she found a way to do something special for mine. What is most disappointing is that Zoë's birthday has always been the day before mine. That year, it was the day that I beat her. She could have gotten the cupcake for herself. Instead, she got one for me.

~

Was it hard for you to digest what happened to Zoë––her death?

Why would it be? If she had half the nightmares I still have to this day, I'm surprised she lasted as long as she did. If it weren't for my children, I probably would have been gone a long time ago. When I think of where my actions could lead them, I remember how my parents not being around landed us in Juby's home, and I change my mind. It's possible Zoë didn't have that–– something to help change her mind in the midst of giving up.

If that statement is true, then you win, right?

What do you mean?

You wanted Zoë to suffer without you. If you could have been that piece she needed to hold on a little longer, and she didn't have it, your plan worked.

I never wanted her to commit suicide though. Maybe I couldn't redeem the time that I lost when I was a kid. Yes, I wanted her to feel what life would be like without me; but I never wanted to lose her––and definitely not like that.

You truly believe Zoë killed herself?

Why wouldn't I? Like I said, I didn't know much about the young adult Zoë, but I could understand how Zoë, the little girl, could end up the way she did. I saw the pain she endured and the scars she covered—physically and mentally. She was a soldier, but many soldiers break—if not during war, it would come after. She wasn't invincible.

What about you? Do you still have thoughts of ending your life?

"What about me?" she asks. Life goes on for me as it always has. My father used to say, "Wha gawn bad a maanin, cyaan cum good a evening."

It means, "What went wrong in the morning cannot be remedied in the evening." I don't waste my energy on times past or on situations I can do nothing about. Zoë was the same way; she just expressed it differently.

And it doesn't matter what my thoughts are about life. I'm still here, healthy, and grateful. There isn't an amount of time long enough to get rid of all the memories. I'm living with them the best I know how.

When was the last time you two were in contact before Zoë died?

Around Christmas the year before. I was preparing to spend the holidays with my husband and our children when Zoë called. She basically said she was down on her luck and needed some place to stay until she sorted out the situation. She briefly mentioned a "guy who went back to his wife" and it all sounded like a huge mess to me. I didn't want her here stirring up drama or causing confusion, so I told her there wasn't enough space with the kids and some of my husband's relatives coming in and out. She seemed to understand. Told me she loved me.

Do you know the names of Zoë's acquaintances? The married guy you mentioned? Anyone?

Besides hearing her talk about her friend, Destiny--who led you to me--the only other name I remember is Marcus. Marcus Pritchard. He's the only guy she ever mentioned to me. He shouldn't be hard to find.

INTERVIEW TWO

Date: Sunday, January 12, 2020
Time: 11:11 AM
Location: Tallahassee, Florida

SOURCE: MARCUS PRITCHARD, JR. AKA M.J.

   I was a redshirted freshman for our basketball team the year she came. I noticed her for the first time after practice that summer. She was hard to miss—unless you just aren't into girls, or your ego can't stomach the possibility of rejection. I remember her dress, not because I'm into chick's clothing, but because it was my favorite color—blue. It wasn't tight, but when she moved I could guess every curve of her body. Oddly, she walked through the student union while reading a book. She moved slow enough to avoid colliding with anything, but she never looked up. I watched her until she reached the end of the sidewalk. When she raised her head to check for traffic, I was caught up. The girl was pretty.

   We passed each other at least once a week that summer. She was always alone, which wasn't weird considering she was new. If it weren't for the guys on the team, I probably would have been the same way. She seemed approachable, but I didn't go near her. Something was unique about this girl, and I was curious, but far from ready to do the work—you know, to figure her out. It was freshman year, and I was becoming well-acclimated to college life—especially the girls.

27

By fall of 2016, I was gearing up to play my first season. I had a head start athletically, and even academically, but I had to balance the academics with my social life since being an athlete couldn't take a backseat to *any*thing.

On the first day of that semester, I was seated in a large lecture hall, so I knew the class would be packed—at least for a week until people started to fall off. It was 10 in the morning, and I had gotten there early. The night before, I slept over at a girl's place on campus; she had to be out by 9, and so was I. I grabbed a breakfast burrito from the union, went to class, and then I waited. People entered one-by-one, or in groups of two or three, wearing flip flops and t-shirts—mostly energized.

The professor came in on the edge of being late, and quickly set up his gear. I was peeling more of the wrapper from my burrito when the door opened, and she walked in. I watched her. She had entered alone, and appeared to ask a few people about seats that were empty near them since the class was almost full. She smiled— *damn*, her smile—as she went row by row scouting for an empty seat. A girl in the middle section waved her hand to get her attention, and she wedged herself between the rows to take her seat.

"Let's begin," the professor said once he was ready. The room was quiet. "Welcome to the first day of fall semester. This is World Religions. We're going to review the course syllabus and guidelines momentarily, but I would first like to take attendance to see if we have any no-shows."

He began to call from the long roster of names, and then it came to me. If I paid attention, I could learn her name. I sat up tall, leaned in, and I watched her. I tried to make it less obvious to the people sitting near me, so my eyes would dart from the professor, back to the girl, and then to some random wall or object in the room. Name after name was called, and still no response from her. She even pulled out a notepad and started writing or doodling, which possibly meant it would be a while.

"Marcus Pritchard," he announced.

I was caught off guard. "That's me," I called out.

A few people giggled. She didn't. Perhaps she didn't hear it.

He continued down his list. I sat back, wanting to abort my plan. "She added the class late and isn't even on the roster. I'm wasting my time," I thought.

"Zoë Sapp," the professor said.

A very gentle voice answered, "I'm here," and she raised her hand into the air.

That was it! I knew her name.

Don't assume anything started between us that day. Again, I wasn't ready to invest, but I had a trick in my arsenal in case she was ever in my vicinity. I would know her name before formally meeting her.

The moment never came. In class, our seats were grandfathered in if you sat there on the first day, so Zoë and I were never closer than four body-filled rows on any given Monday, Wednesday, or Friday that I chose to show up.

We reached finals week at the end of the semester, and I don't believe I had ever opened the book. I could buy the study notes easily, so that was my plan. First, I had to stop by Strozier, the main library in the center of campus, to pick up a book I needed for a research paper in another course.

The library was bursting at its seams. There were wall-to-wall study groups, people sprawled out in the middle of the floor or hidden between bookshelves for a quiet space. I found the book I needed in the stacks, and was heading to check it out when I saw her—Zoë. Again, she was alone and sitting in one of the comfortable, decorative chairs—no paper, pens, textbooks, or notebooks in sight. Her hair was usually pulled up, but her curls dangled loosely over her eyes, which parted in places, and she looked through them to read the paperback book she held in her hands. I was prepared to pass her just as we had done for over a year, but she looked up from her book, and saw me.

I nodded as if to say, "What's up?"

She shook her head and shrugged her shoulders as if to say, "Nothing much."

I laughed, and it loosened me up enough to approach her.

She didn't budge in her chair, fluff her hair, or press her lips together to check her gloss—you know, the stuff girls do when they're interested in a guy. She just laid her book against her chest and looked at me.

"Hey," she said.

"Hey Zoë," I responded. I was ready to impress her.

"Are you here to study too?" she asked.

I failed. She wasn't impressed, and didn't ask how I knew her name, but I sucked it up and kept the conversation going.

"Yeah. I guess. I really came to pick up this book, but I might try to slide into one of these groups."

"For which class?"

"The one I have with you," was my second attempt.

"World Religions."

She knew *me*.

"How did you know?"

"I have eyes."

If she knew that, it was possible that she also knew my name. "Know my name too?" I flashed her a smile.

"How could I? You didn't tell me."

Damn.

"It's Marcus."

"Cool. Nice to meet you." She extended her hand to touch me. Our hands connected briefly.

"What are you studying?" I asked her.

"Nothing," she shrugged a single shoulder.

"But it's finals week."

"I know. I'm taking finals this week," she said with enormous sarcasm. I chuckled.

"So, you're *not* studying."

"I know all I'm going to know." She moved the book down from her chest and leaned towards me. "Is that what you think these people are doing?" She sat up and looked at the sea of students spread around the room. The only vacant spaces were on the tops of bookshelves.

"Yeah. It's *finals* week."

"They're not studying; they're cramming."

"Same difference."

"Not at all."

A girl walked away from the table where she sat a few feet from us, and I found an opportunity to extend the moment. I quickly grabbed the chair and placed it in front of Zoë's.

"Tell me how," I said.

"Ooookay."

"What? I thought you were about to school me on the difference between *cramming* and *studying*. I didn't want you to keep looking up at me while you spoke."

"Nice of you, but nope. I was done when I suggested there was a difference. Reasonable doubt zone. Class over."

She had incredible range. She could go from sweet to sarcasm to witty and back to sweet before she drove a single point home. And when she spoke, she kept her eyes casually locked on the person she was talking to—not in a way that was scary, or weird. Her gesture emphasized the fact that she was addressing you—and you alone. Her eyes didn't wander nervously or search the space above her head for the right words to say. She just said them, and watched how others responded.

"Okay. Well, since you're ready for the test, can you help

me?"

"I'm not a tutor." Her thumb continued to hold her place in the book she had been reading—as if our interaction would soon be over and she would get back to it.

"I know. Maybe you can tell me what you think my notes are missing."

"If you're like half the students in that class, and only show up on occasion, I can tell you that your notes are missing a nice chunk without looking at them."

"Then let me see yours."

"That's what this is? You want my notes?"

"No, I can buy notes. I want your help."

She smirked, and paused a moment. *Got her.*

She removed her thumb from the book, closed it, reached for her shoulder bag, and pulled out a thick, spiral notebook. On the outside, she had drawn flowers, the shapes of birds, and a few misplaced ocean waves. I tossed the book I carried to the floor and took off my book bag, which was bare. I wore it most days to avoid having to lug anything around campus in my hands. Some days, it only contained a single set of keys.

I pulled out a thin notebook, and was immediately embarrassed as I shuffled through the pages. I didn't know if I should risk her seeing the mere four pages of notes from a full semester of lectures. I kept shuffling even when I got to the inkless pages. I hadn't planned that far ahead. My "situations" with other girls didn't include them having any insight into my academic life. Watching me on the court, burgers and fries, some late-night creeping, was typically the full extent of it.

"Let me see your notes," she said.

"Wait. Before you look at—."

She playfully snatched the notebook from my hands.

"I don't do disclaimers." She started to turn the pages and read over my writing.

"Look, it's been crazy. I started my first season and—."

"*Shh.* I'm reading your notes," she said, and then immediately closed the notebook. "Done."

I laughed. "I know. Bad, right? I think I have more notes in my phone though." I pulled my phone from my back pocket and intended to look for the notes I had taken. Instead, notifications of unread text messages and Instagram alerts flashed across the screen, and didn't think twice before checking them.

"I mean—you can use my notes. Make a copy if it would help," she said.

31

I tried to quickly swipe through the notifications to get back to her, but it was taking longer than I expected.

Zoë continued, "Or if my notes aren't to your liking, you can still buy them across campus."

I knew she was looking, but I was near finished, and would soon get to my notes.

"You could choose either of them, but they won't help you," she said.

I was lost in a text a teammate sent about a girl we'd met at a party, and had only partly heard what she'd said. "What was that?" I asked.

"Nothing."

"Wait." I played the moment back. "Did you just say I'll fail?"

"No. I said the notes won't help."

I looked back down at my phone—for just a second.

"There is your problem. Another junkie."

"What?" She had my attention.

"Phones, social media. Addiction. Most people can't focus because of them——."

"I'm not always on my phone."

"Define *always*. While taking showers, sleeping, or playing basketball don't count either."

"Damn."

"If you have to set an intention to stay away something, sounds like you're pretty hooked."

"I can't agree with that."

"Of course not."

"It's just how you see things."

"Yeah. I guess my lens is a little advanced." If she hadn't said it with a smile, it's possible I would have been offended.

"Wow. Okay," was all I could muster.

"Come on. Why do you think they call paid members *influencers*? People are under the influence of something whether they know it or not." With that, she pulled the novel back out of her bag.

"Whatever. I bet you're the selfie queen."

"Nah. A picture doesn't do me any justice. The Zoë experience is expensive." She started to shuffle through the book's pages.

"Really? What it cost?"

She rested the book on her lap. "Time. The only resource that can't be replenished. This," she pointed to herself, "is expensive. Social media drives down the value of being in my presence."

"So, what? You got a few investors?"

"Only a few, but again, if I set my value high enough, I can weed out the ones that aren't willing to stretch themselves or sacrifice to be near me. And that's Marketing 101—passed it with flying colors."

"I see what you're saying."

"Clicking the 'like' button on a picture will never compare to 'you're beautiful' being whispered in my ear."

~

Did the two of you date officially? Were you in a relationship?

I don't know what the average person would call what Zoë and I had, but she wasn't the average girl. Calling her "different" would be an understatement. We were friends. She was a *really* good friend.

You were intimate then.

Wait. I was sincere when I said we were close, if you thought I was hinting at something else. She truly became a good friend to me.

It's frustrating to sit here and try to find the words to describe the person she was. She was kind and giving—yes—but she also liked to be in control; but not in control of other people. She liked to be in control of herself. I know it sounds crazy for me to complain about her having self-control, but I don't know if she understood how it affected the people around her. She did everything on her own terms, and in her own time. People either got with it, or they didn't, and either way she wasn't moved.

So, you weren't intimate?

Yes, we had sex. I don't usually hesitate to talk about who I've been with. I'm a grown ass man now--getting ready to graduate and all. I'm far from shy; but I can't reduce what I had with Zoë to "just sex." She wasn't.

Then tell me what you liked most about her.

Aside from her honesty, I came to appreciate how genuine her motives were. I mean-- everyone is out to get something, or become somebody. We look at people and opportunities like stepping stones--step on and pass by. With Zoë, you could visibly see what she was doing, but her actions scratched beyond the surface of her ego.

She was in this leadership club on campus at one point. I know she joined a group of poets too. She didn't join organizations to fluff her resume or build contacts. No matter where she went, or what she was doing, she had a way of connecting with people. Zoë wasn't one to try and make a name for herself or have the spotlight. She really wanted to help people--especially troubled kids. She volunteered with the kids in juvie like it was a part-time job.

Why do you think she spent so much time there?

On paper, she was an English major, but she wanted to study law after undergrad. Zoë wanted to defend kids who got caught up in the system, especially those who had faced different adversities in their upbringing.

She would say, "Poor people can't afford to be victims."

For a while, I was all over the place, so it wasn't until she died that I understood what she meant. No one feels sorry for the kid who is a victim of circumstance, poverty, violence, or abandonment and finds him or herself facing the consequences of a bad decision. Instead, they're punished and robbed of any shot at normalcy and stability.

Zoë even said she would do it for free. Crazy, right? With the amount of time she would invest into getting her degree, and all the student loan debt that would pile up, I couldn't understand. She told me she could live off the fulfillment her work would bring alone, but that didn't give me any more clarity.

~

Zoë was a cool chick. We didn't share any classes after that fall semester, but we started to connect during Union Wednesdays when it began to warm up outside. We made small talk between classes.

One day, we were tucked off behind one of the cement columns while we watched one of the modeling troupes give us a preview of their upcoming show.

"You could do that," she said as one of the male models walked out and popped his collar.

"I'm almost 6'6". I only see the shorter guys doing stuff like this."

"Anyone can do it."

"But it's good to know you think I'm cute."

She blushed. "Don't let it go to your head."

"Oooo. But she didn't disagree! Now we're getting somewhere."

"Whatever."

Someone walked by and handed her a flyer. She read it silently and then handed it over to me.

"It's a party. You trying to go?" I asked her.

"Nah. I'm good."

"It's the Black Student Union though."

"Don't act like you go to those parties."

"What? I don't—but they might be straight though."

"Yeah, I'm straight on it too."

"You got something against the BSU?"

"No. But I think it's pretty obvious that I'm black."

"More like hazelnut, but I'll hear you out," I joked.

"Shut up!" she laughed. "I really don't see the benefit of singling myself out just to connect with others based on a single commonality."

"That's different."

"I'm a fly in a glass of milk in most of my classes. Emphasizing my blackness is just an invitation to be perceived and treated like I'm not just as good, or intelligent, as anyone else on every other level."

"So, your black ain't beautiful?"

"What's with the jokes today, dude?" She nudged my arm. "Yeah, it is, but so is what's inside me."

I raised an eyebrow at her suggestively. "Inside, huh?"

She looked at the invisible watch on her wrist. "Was that the bell? I'm about to leave your ass right here. You play too much."

"Who said I'm playing?" She started to walk away and I pulled her back. "Okay. I'm playing." She relaxed back into her position. "I saw a video on my timeline a while ago. It was a lady named Julia Hare. She said, 'Integration is the illusion of inclusion.'"

"Who said I wanted to be included? Society's need to meet affirmative action quotas have nothing to do with actual college life. What I'll experience here, and anywhere I go, is completely up to me. I'm here because I choose to be—even when I don't feel included."

"You wouldn't care if you felt like you didn't belong?"

"I never belong. My high school was filled with people who looked like me; I didn't belong there either. Going across the tracks won't suddenly make me more accepted," she said. "I won't busy myself with finding ways to feel accepted by other people. Not with all it took to finally accept myself. I would spend a lifetime convincing people that I'm good, or smart, or pretty. Fuck it. I'm me. By the time people understand that, their season is up anyway. Why bother."

"So, you don't agree with Julia Hare?"

"I do. In high school, my favorite teacher was a white woman who taught American History. I admired her, and I wanted to attend her alma mater. When I told her I had applied, I thought she would be excited. Instead, she told me I had a better chance of getting in because I was black. She didn't tell me how smart or deserving I was. She only considered my race. I got into that school, but I didn't go. It's fine if others believe I'm only here because someone extended a favor, but I know the truth. My academic record could rival most of the students here regardless of their race."

"All I'm saying is the Black Student Union might be a good space to connect with like-minded people—make friends."

"No one is like-minded."

"What about the girl you said you hang out with—your old roommate? Not even her?"

"No. We're not, but it's not a good or a bad thing. We agree on enough to be good friends, and cling to each other a little tighter when our friendship is challenged by our differences."

I understood Zoë's perspective. I realized she liked to be close enough to feel connected, but not so close to be attached—not even the girl that she had told me the week before was her *best* friend.

"Would you say *we* agree on enough for me to—umm—get your number?"

"Well, I'll be damned. The rookie has finally grown some balls," she said before adding her contact to my device. It was not the response I expected, and far from flattering, but it was her personality. Some might say it was tasteless, and that girls should say *this* or do *that*, but Zoë was real—not like the ones who angelically blush, grin and comply if I said I just wanted to fuck. Zoë didn't care what anyone thought of what she would say as long as she knew it was coming from a good place. Somehow, she had truly learned her worth, and gave me a hard time for just asking for a damn phone number. It wasn't a game of cat and mouse. She was right. I could have asked for her number an entire year before, but I didn't have the nerve.

Like social media, Zoë wasn't big on texting. Hours would go by without a response from her—if not days. And she kept her responses short when she sent them. Typically, she would only text if she 1) couldn't talk at that moment, **and** 2) was arranging to actually see you in person. At first, we didn't chat much at all, and saw each other even less.

When I was sixteen, my parents gave their consent for me to get tattooed. It's the thing to do where I'm from, so it was more typical to see a high schooler working towards completing a sleeve than receiving a diploma. By freshman year, I was up to eight tattoos between both arms and my chest, and I had room for plenty more. I was in the middle of working on my largest tattoo—a roaring lion on my upper back. The process was painful, and varied by the section of the back the artist was tattooing. The outline was set, and my second session of shading was sure to be a doozie.

On the day of my appointment, I sat in the waiting area until the artist wrapped up a previous client when, out the blue, Zoë text me to see what I was doing. The tattoo artist was the best in the city, and my appointments had been set and paid for months in advance, so I wasn't dipping out on it. I also didn't want to miss a chance to see her, so I told her where I was and asked if she wanted to come through. Surprisingly, she did.

When she arrived about a half hour later, I was already face-down on the artist's table, but I turned my head to see her. She wore a pair of jeans and a shirt with triangle graphics on the front. Her hair was pulled high, and her perfume lit up the room when she walked in.

"Hey, stranger," she said.

"What up?" I responded.

"Hey, I'm Tony," the tattoo artist said as he shook her hand.

Zoë checked out the work on my back. "Dope. Looks like it hurts."

"Like shit," I told her.

She found a chair in the corner of the room and sat down. "Obviously, it's worth the pain or you wouldn't do it."

"I guess. I'm in it for what it looks like when it's done. Fuck all the pain."

"I'm sure no one wants to deal with pain. But I guess when it comes to tattoos, the result is a masterpiece."

"Not all of 'em. I've seen some bad work. Right, Tony?"

"Yeah. In a college town like this one, a lot of kids want quick, cheap tats. There are shops that'll give it to 'em too. And that's exactly what they look like—quick and cheap," Tony said.

"But not my dude here."

"You're one of the best, huh?" Zoë asked.

"I've been an artist all my life. I'm almost 45. I've been in the business for over 20 years. People who come to me want quality work."

"Yeah, and you gotta book him almost six months in advance."

"Good problem to have for me, bro."

Zoë noticed the picture book on the counter next to her and she picked it up. She slowly turned the pages and gazed at Tony's work. "These are good. Your shading technique—wow. How long will it take to finish his back?"

"This is our third session. We should be done after tonight."

"Shit. I hope so. I'm ready to be done with this," I said, and then clenched my teeth as the needle dug into my skin. I loosened the tension in my forehead so that Zoë couldn't see the pain in my face.

The three of us talked for two hours about one topic or another. Zoë had moments where she would stand up to check his progress, and flatter him with compliments. At least twice during the session, Tony stepped outside for a smoke break, and Zoë and I were alone in the room.

"How you feelin', kid?" she asked during Tony's second break.

I sat up on the bed to stretch a little before he returned. "I'm good. Hungry."

"Me too. You want me to grab something for you?" She checked out my back. "He's only halfway there."

"Nah. I don't want to eat in here."

"You just might be bougie."

"Me?" I chuckled. "Nah. I just want to get this shit over with. I don't have the patience for more breaks. It hurts."

"Sure don't look like it."

"Believe me."

Tony walked back into the room. "Ready to finish up?" he asked.

"Let's get it." I laid flat on the table again.

"What time does the studio close tonight, Tony?" Zoë asked.

"10," he answered. "M. J. will wrap it up for me tonight."

"Is it possible to make room for one more?" she asked. I was caught completely off-guard.

"For who?" Tony asked. "You?"

Zoë smiled. "I know you have a process, but I figured it wouldn't hurt to ask."

He pressed the needle to my skin. "What you getting?" he asked.

"Nothing big. Maybe the size of a deck of cards."

"I would have to sketch something for you and everything. Tonight wouldn't work."

"I don't want you to sketch it."

"You want to use something you've already seen before?"

"Freehand it. I trust you."

"What do you want him to freehand, Zoë?" I chimed in.

"A phoenix. Grayscale. Nothing fancy."

"That's a popular tattoo. I've probably done hundreds of them over the years."

"Yeah. But how many did you freehand?" she asked.

"None."

"Why do you want a phoenix?" I asked her.

"Probably for the same reason you're getting a fuckin' lion on your back." She laughed.

"I'm the king in these streets. Ask about me."

"Boy, shut up," she said playfully. "I like the phoenix."

"You must have gone through some shit. Most of the girls who come in here to get them survived some dark times," Tony said. The tattoo gun buzzed near my ear.

"That wouldn't be my reason. The phoenix is immortal. It constantly rises."

"That's one way to see it." There was silence as Tony stuck the needle into the paint. "I won't promise, but let me check the time when I'm done with him. I may be able to get you in before I head out."

Zoë smiled. "Okay. Thank you." She sat back in her chair and continued to browse the images in Tony's portfolio.

After another hour of chatter, and the completion of my artwork, Tony had determined he could squeeze Zoë in if she was ready with $200. For work of his quality, that was a steal. I believe he had taken a liking to Zoë to have extended himself to do an impromptu tat for so cheap.

She wanted the artwork on her right side, about an inch below her boobs. For it, she removed her shirt. Her bra was lace, and dark tan. It almost blended with her skin. I wanted to catch a full view of her breasts, but once she removed her shirt, she covered them with her arms. He had her sit backwards in a chair, which covered her front even more. Instead, I admired the smoothness of her back—especially the dimples in the lower region that sat right above her jeans.

Tony gathered the paint and other materials, and put on a fresh pair of gloves. I was so hungry that I wanted to run out for something to eat, but I couldn't leave her in there—shirtless. I sat in the chair and watched.

"Will it hurt?" she asked after she heard the buzz of the gun.

"Yes," he said.

"Damn, you won't even sugarcoat it for me?"

"Nope."

40

"I appreciate your honesty. Let's do it then."

He pressed the needle into her skin, and she immediately looked down at it, which caused her body to jerk.

"Don't move. You gotta sit really still."

She did as she was told. She didn't move, and she didn't speak either. Tony and I carried on a conversation as if she wasn't in the room. Her skin began to glisten and, on occasion, she would let out a gentle moan.

It was almost 10:30 and other artists were cleaning and preparing to leave. Zoë's work had taken almost two hours to complete, but when he finished, it was amazing. He had colored the phoenix in various shades of gray. Instead of fire, it appeared that the phoenix was rising through a scattered cloud of smoke, which gripped its tail. It was nothing short of magical.

She looked at herself in the mirror, and smirked.

"You like it?" Tony asked.

"Understatement of the year. You're a beast," she said.

"Good," Tony said as he cleaned up his area. "Let me wrap you up."

He covered Zoë's tattoo and gave her instructions to care for it before we thanked him and left the studio.

"You still hungry?" I asked Zoë.

"Yes. Let's grab some tacos," she suggested.

"Yeah, but none of that tofu shit you were eating in the union."

We opened the door to exit, and the light of the full moon was brighter than any I had experienced before. It caused Zoë to stop in her tracks. She was mesmerized by it.

"Wow," she said as she stared at its enormity. She closed her eyes and inhaled deeply.

After a while, she opened her eyes to witness my awkward gaze.

"What?" she said.

"You like the moon, huh?" I said as we approached our cars, which were parked next to each other.

"I love the moon. It's so refreshing. What's wrong with that?"

"It's weird. Isn't it the thing witches worship? I thought you believed in God?"

"What? Are you serious? I love all creation, and its Creator—including the moon. God is—God is in everything…sun, moon, stars, trees, birds, you, me—everything."

I was puzzled.

"Come here," she said, and grabbed my shoulders. She touched the edge of my freshly-tattooed skin, and I flinched. "I'm sorry. Didn't mean to hurt you."

"It's cool. You didn't."

She continued to position my shoulders—but more gently.

"Close your eyes. Breathe in as deep as you can. Let the light of the moon wash over you. You feel that?"

"What am I supposed to be feeling right now?"

"Peace. Clarity, maybe."

"You're not trying to get me into your moon worship shit, are you?"

"Whatever. I appreciate the moon, it's splendor and energy, but I don't worship it. I stop and listen to you. Take in every word you say. I appreciate you, and what you've shared with me. By your standard, I must worship you too."

"I'm not saying that. What's the point of appreciating the moon. It's just the moon."

"I never knew there was such a thing as being too grateful. I appreciate the things I never want to lose."

"So what if we lost the moon."

"You really didn't listen in Earth Space Science."

"I mean—I did. Wait. You said you appreciate things you don't want to lose."

"Yeah. Everything."

"You said you appreciate *me*."

"Why would I want to lose you?" she smirked.

~

Do you believe Zoë loved you?

Zoë loved everything. She never spoke the words before, but I know she cared about me. I've heard girls say they love me after a week of smashing, but it wasn't the same as when Zoë *showed* it. It's like--she didn't say it, she became it, and everything and everyone she encountered was able to sense it.

Did you love her?

I was a sophomore. I felt something for her, but I don't throw out the "L" word unless you're mom dukes. I liked her more than any of the other girls I came across. I didn't have a lot of downtime, but I spent the time I had with Zoë whenever she was open to it. Other chicks could only join me during sleeping hours, which didn't cause me to sacrifice anything.

Can you take me back to one of the most memorable times you shared with Zoë?

You asked if Zoë and I were intimate, and I got in my feelings a little bit. I'm sorry about that. We had sex. Once. And although I want to say it's one of my biggest regrets, I'll just say it was one of my greatest lessons.

~

I spent most of my time in class, practice, or at away games, but Zoë was a busybody who despised routines. She would take random trips to the park, museums, workshops, movie theaters, rallies, conferences—anything to keep her moving between classes and volunteering at the juvenile detention center. If all else failed, you could find her in the library *not* studying, of course, but reading leisurely. Or, on good-weather days, you might roll up on her sleeping in a canoe in the middle of Lake Bradford. I've never actually seen her do it, but she told me about a time when she was so relaxed soaking up the sun that she fell asleep. Fortunately for her, the melanin in her skin prevented the experience from becoming a painful one. She stayed out there until The Rez was about to close. One of the staff members had to row out to what they thought was an abandoned canoe and found her there—still asleep.

I'm not one for sun and water, but our thing was going to the movies. It was the one activity that had a cost of admission every day of the week, so Zoë couldn't take advantage of some promotional "get in free" day. I'd always foot the bill and, on average, we went once a week. On Thursdays, we would catch a matinee since neither of us had class before 3 o'clock. We usually grabbed something to eat before or after, but nothing fancy—food court fare or the Chinese buffet across the street from the mall. Some would say we were dating, but we didn't call it anything.

I couldn't resist hitting her with sexual innuendos and random references to various body parts, or hugging her tightly to share in the warmth of her body, or the urge to invite her over so we could "chill". She was cool with all of that, and we would indeed "chill", but we weren't having sex. We went on this way until summer—a full semester with no play (from her anyway). Although I was putting my best foot forward, I wasn't sprung on her, so it was nothing to invite someone over who could help me "reset". I had established a reputation on campus as an athlete, and at my height, I'm hard to miss. It was nothing to be noticed—and even easier to bring someone home with me. And I did—often.

I tried to talk myself out of calling or texting Zoë a few times. I knew the situation with her was going nowhere, or at least not in the direction I wanted it to go—with her naked in my bed. Then I would remember her smile, the way she always smelled like the cake batter my grandmother whipped up from scratch when I was a kid—sugar and almond—and I would find myself hopeful enough to see her again. I walked a tight rope, and it was hard to settle on what I really wanted from her.

I had some downtime one Saturday night, so I grabbed a movie from Redbox and called Zoë over. She was a sucker for chips and salsa, and an even bigger sucker for fresh guacamole, so I promised her dip if she would come over.

She must have just gotten out of the shower when I called because she was at my place within 15 minutes, and her hair was soaked—and so was the t-shirt she wore. It was faded, and the print was almost gone. The collar had been ripped, so it hung loosely from one of her shoulders. Beads of oil and water from her hair would cascade down her collar bone and into the area she wouldn't permit me to see. Within 20 minutes of *Get Out*, the dripping ceased, and I was no longer tormented by my curiosity—so I thought.

I sat on the couch with my legs propped on the center table, but I wanted to stretch out.

"Slide down to the end," I told her.

As she moved down, she tugged at her gym shorts, which had risen up her thigh more than she was comfortable. I laid my head in her lap, and my legs fell over the arm of the couch.

"Damn, Jolly Green Giant," she said. "Either you need to stop growing, or to tell your roommates that y'all need a longer couch."

"Ha ha. I definitely need a new couch with all this Soul Glo you got dripping on it."

"Whatever." She removed a hair tie from her wrist. "I just wanted it to dry a little bit before I pulled it up."

My phone vibrated on the table; I reached for it to turn it off.

"Oh, I get undivided attention tonight." She grabbed a plain tortilla chip and crunched on it.

"You might be special," I joked.

"Then you should tell *her* that."

"You serious?"

"About what?"

"About another girl being on my phone."

"I don't care who's on your phone. Watch the movie."

"Because you don't care or...?" I was curious.

"Listen, even if I cared, I don't ask questions I won't take pleasure in knowing the answer to." Her eyes stayed on the screen as she spoke. It was unlike her to not look at me. The message was very clear. She did not want to have the discussion.

"That's weird as fuck." I nestled my head in her lap. A part of me wanted to pick a fight with Zoë—if for nothing else, for kicks. I didn't care about her lack of concern for who was calling me. What man would raise the topic of his personal phone to *any* woman? We would rather they not even know we owned one; and if they did, we'd pretend our shit was invisible, and our ringers were like dog whistles.

She finally looked at me. "Damn, boy. It feels like you're digging a hole with your big ass head. Be still! It is *my* lap. And I'll forgive the fact that you just called me 'weird'. Do you even know how often you use that word? A lot. And that's weird."

"But you are. Don't forget—'as fuck.'"

"Someone like you would dog a woman if she accused you of being with other women. But here I am trying to eat my salsa and chips in peace and shit, and you pop-off because I don't give a fuck about it. And *I'm* weird."

"Perhaps that's it. Maybe you should finally give a fuck," I said.

"Okay. This seems like a totally different conversation. So, this is not about another chick?" she asked.

"Nah. It's about me."

"You think cussing your ass out over another chick calling or texting you proves I care about you? Why?"

I didn't want to respond. My behavior was definitely stupid once she put it that way.

She spoke passionately, "If you can't sense what I feel for you through each of your nerve endings and down to your bones, I don't know what to tell you."

"Well, I don't. I try to get close to you sometimes, or touch you, and you—."

"Again, total misdirect. This isn't even about me caring for you. Is it? It's about sex."

"Could be." I was too invested into getting what I wanted to deny it.

"Okay. So, you wanna fuck?"

I didn't know if it was a trick question.

"I haven't held back anything. If that's it, say it," she said.

"Yeah."

"Got it. I respect that."

Zoë quietly sat back and began to watch the movie again.

"You don't want to?" I asked.

"No. I do," she responded with her eyes focused on the television.

For a moment, I was relieved and thought that we both wanted the same thing.

"What? We have to be married or something?"

She laughed. "Nah. I'm not a virgin, or waiting for marriage to do it again."

"Sometimes I see you a few times a week and—." It hit me that she could have someone else. "Hold up. You got a dude?"

"No, silly. It would make the time I spend with you cheating."

"Then what?"

"It's hard to explain."

"You always find a way. Shoot."

"There have been guys I've slept with—fewer than the fingers on both hands if you're wondering—and then there are guys I've connected with, and we became friends. I've never had both with one person."

"How the hell did I land on the friend side?"

"You wanna go to the other side?"

"Yeah."

"At the expense of never returning to this one?"

"What?"

"I mean it." She breathed deeply. "My feelings for you are obvious. I gave that away. My body, sex, is something I've kept out of this situation. I can't give you both."

I read the sincerity in her face. "You serious." I sat up and moved close to her. "Damn. I have to choose?"

"Or, we can pretend we didn't have this conversation."

I was curious to know what it was like on the other side, and I was confident her little speech was bullshit. I moved my hand to her thigh. She inhaled deeply, but didn't move. After a moment, she placed her hand on top of mine and guided it further up her thigh as she gazed into my eyes. I leaned in and kissed her, and she gently cuffed my ears and pulled me closer. Our bodies must have maneuvered themselves because, before I knew it, I was completely on top of her and could sense the warmth of her sweet spot through her shorts; and she had no choice but to feel me too—pressed firmly against her, grinding slowly.

I tugged at her shorts, wanting her to take them off, and she stopped my hand. I backed out of the kiss, and foolishly thought she was about to rob me of my rightful option.

"Are you sure?" she asked. No one had ever asked *me* before.

I didn't answer. I started to kiss her again to indicate my response, and still believed it was some silly game she played to not seem easy. She finally let go. I pulled her shirt over her head, and squeezed her breasts before I lowered her bra to kiss and suck all over them. My lips moved down to her freshly-healed tattoo, and the experience we shared that evening flashed quickly into my thoughts; but the warmth and scent of her body brought me back into the present instantly.

In the intensity of the moment, I had forgotten I didn't live alone. When I realized we were in the living room, and she was half-naked, I wanted to hide her away—not to satisfy my need for privacy, but to protect her. I took her by the hand and walked her into my bedroom.

It was dark, but the lamp post outside provided enough light for us to get around. Zoë had never been in my bedroom, but she wasn't distracted by posters of basketball legends on my wall, or my mismatched bedding. Fortunately, it was clean. When she entered, she immediately sat on the bed and removed her bra completely. Her breasts were large, and perfectly round. I took off my shirt as I stood in front of her. Her hands caressed my abs and she kissed around my navel as much as she could with my penis protruding through my basketball shorts. The excitement caused me to lift her by her arms and move her to the center of the bed. I dropped my shorts and underwear, reached inside the nightstand for a condom, and put it on as she watched. And that night, we finally did it.

Before I knew it, the sun was rising. We had fallen asleep so quickly that the rubber was still on the floor beside the bed, and we were both still naked. The soft light in the room made her skin glow. She slept so peacefully that I didn't want to wake her, but I won't deny the thought of a second round with her.

I reached over and grabbed my shorts from the floor to get my phone. It was only 7 o'clock. There was a message from one of my coaches that was sent the night before, and I immediately began to respond. I don't know how long she had been awake, or watching, but Zoë tossed the covers aside and sprang from the bed, giving me a mere flash of her fully nude body in daylight. *Exceptional.*

"Wait. Where you going?" I asked.

"Home." She pulled up her panties.

I looked at the phone in my hand, and assumed she believed I would text another woman while she was in bed with me.

"This isn't—I mean—I'm responding to my coach. I'm..."

"I told you; I don't care." She slid her shorts up her thighs.

"Then why are you leaving? It's Sunday."

She looked at me as she pulled her shirt over her head, but didn't respond.

"Alright then. If you wanna do the movies or just hang out later, I got you."

"Mm hm. Yeah." She walked out of the room.

I heard her grab her keys, and the front door slam shut, but she didn't say anything more.

I called her a few times that week, sent text messages, but they went unanswered. Summer session had started, but I didn't know what classes she was taking, so I couldn't go there. I stopped by her place, only once, but no one came to the door. I wasn't registered for any classes that session, so I wasn't on campus long enough to catch her in passing. It finally hit me that Zoë's ultimatum was real. I thought about her, but time softens the suffering of missing someone.

After we crossed into Summer C, I had completed a workout and was walking out of the Leach Center when I saw a familiar face coming towards me. It took a moment to process how I wanted to respond, or prepare for how she would respond to me, but she smiled, and I was reminded. She was dressed in workout gear, and her hair was pulled up from her face. I held the door open for her to walk inside.

"Hey," was all I could say.

"Hey, Marcus," she said pleasantly and slowed her pace.

"You been alright?"

"Yeah. Good. You?" she asked.

"Yeah. It's been cool."

"Good."

There was a puzzling silence.

"Hope you had a good workout. See you later." She walked away, and was gone again.

It was the summer of 2017. She had meant what she said. Although I would spot her on campus on occasion, we were never friends again.

~

You seem upset after sharing that. Do you need a moment?

No. I'm good. Most people would say I was in the "friend zone" all along--like I had imagined some relationship between me and Zoë. That's not true. When we were together, everything about her showed me she wanted something more. I still find it hard to rest on the fact that she just didn't know how-- or that she was too afraid to try.

This is college. And you said it yourself, there were a lot of girls. Could that have anything to do with it?

At first, I didn't believe Zoë was genuine when she said she didn't care about me being with other girls. There are women who say it, but eventually the truth seeps out when they're going through your shit, or watching your eyes when another girl walks by. But Zoë never did that. She focused so much on the moment that she didn't have time to think of anything, or anyone, that wasn't sharing it with her. And she was on the go so much that I'm sure she would never have the time to entertain suspicions. If she wanted to know something, she could ask me. She knew that, but never did.

Do you think she would have eventually learned to be in a committed relationship?

She told me she had *never* had a boyfriend, but she didn't say she never wanted one. She also didn't say she wanted one *someday*. A relationship wasn't a necessity for her like it is for most people. She managed relationships like a yo-yo. She'd wind you up and bring you in real tight, and then release you--sometimes to dangle for a while. After we had sex, she completely cut the string.

I have to ask you: Did you ever think Zoë would take her own life?

Zoë was levelheaded, strong, in control. To me, she was healthy and happy in every way, but incredibly different. I'm not a shrink. I can't say there were any warning signs that would make me think this could happen to her. I knew she was different, but to me, her type of different made her "good." And it's hard to imagine that people as good as her would kill themselves.

Did she ever talk about her past?

Come to think of it--no, not really.

Do you know where Zoë grew up?

No. I don't.

What about her parents?

She never talked about them.

Did you ever ask?

I think I know where this is going. It's possible that I didn't know enough about her to say she wouldn't kill herself.

I can't begin to explain how Zoë redefined so many things for me. The traditional sense of "knowing" someone is not the type of "knowing" you would have with Zoë. She kept her conversations in the present, and she learned what she needed to know about you when you were *in* her presence. It isn't about some generic "getting to know you" formula, or Q&A sessions, like we had on the phone until 3 AM back in high school. Zoë's behaviors, her level of understanding—-and not just for a girl her age, but for people in general—-was completely alien. And that's the only way I can describe it.

Is there anything more you'd like to tell me about Zoë?

In a traditional sense, all I knew about her was that she had a sister, but how I found out was unusual.

Tell me how you discovered she had a sister.

Zoë was at my place one evening. Her car was giving her trouble, and she needed a ride to the grocery store. We were each other's taxi driver on any given day, so it was nothing to me. I went to my room to change clothes and left my phone on the living room table. I heard the chirp of a Facebook notification. I didn't use the app often, but someone had tagged me in a photo. She asked to see it, and I thought she wanted to see the picture, but she clicked the "x" instead and moved the phone closer. I sat next to her on the sofa and put on my shoes, but I wanted to keep an eye on what she was doing. She pressed the screen a few times and her thumbs started to type. She clicked and scrolled for a while, and I got a little nervous thinking she was going through my phone. Before I could make up some excuse for her to hand it back to me, she put it down on the table.

We left for the store, and Zoë was quiet-- almost sad. Sass and sarcasm were totally muted. I asked what was wrong, and she insisted she was okay. She perked up a little before I dropped her off at home, but the vibe was still a little off.

When I reopened the app and checked my history, she had searched for a woman with the same last name as hers. The profile picture of the woman resembled Zoë, but she could have been a little older. There were pictures of the woman with who I assumed was her husband and their kids; a few pictures with some tagged friends at various events; some pictures with co-workers wearing medical scrubs; and random artwork. I wanted to confirm she and Zoë were related, so I browsed nearly all the woman's pictures—-but there were none of Zoë.

EXHIBIT ONE: Zoë's Canopy Road

Date: Monday, January 13, 2020
Time: 5:45 PM
Location: Tallahassee, Florida

Interview Three

Date: Monday, January 13, 2020
Time: 3:16 PM
Location: Tallahassee, Florida

SOURCE: DESTINY WILLIAMS

How did you and Zoë meet?

We both started in the summer bridge program in 2015. Everyone in the program was newbies fresh out of their mama's houses, and nervous about starting college. I was running late on move-in day because my uncle decided to get his slow ass car serviced at the time we were supposed to hit the road. No one wants to walk into a new environment *and* be the last to get there, so I was anxious.

One of the counselors handed my keys over, and I raced up to my assigned room. As I stepped off the elevator, I started to check the door numbers, and calculated that my new dorm room was about two or three doors down the hall—-and exactly where a white woman stood. She had a cane in her hand, and she

57

leaned against the wall—-waiting. At first I thought, "Oh shit! I got a white-girl roommate." Nothing against them; it just would have all been new to me. The lady introduced herself and said that my new roommate, Zoë, had gone downstairs to get something from the car and that she was coming right back.

I stepped inside the room. I assumed if my roommate had gotten there before me, she would choose her bed first and get all her shit set up before I walked in to take whatever was left over. At least, *I* would have done that; but Zoë's things were still stacked neatly near the front door. I thought to call dibs before she came back, but after giving it a second thought, I dropped my bag in the middle of the room. I would give her the same courtesy she had given me.

I was shocked when she came in though. Of course, I assumed she was white, but here was a chick who looked like Gabrielle Union and Rihanna's love child. She immediately hugged me—-tight. Zoë asked which side of the room I wanted, and I felt obligated to let her choose first. She did.

Did you two party a lot when you started here?

Me, definitely. There wasn't a party or night club that I didn't sample when I first got here. Zoë, not so much. The girl wasn't a lame—-well actually, compared to the average college student, she was pretty lame; but she wasn't self-righteous. Even if she didn't want to go certain places with me, she would stay up late to hear me talk about it when I got back.

I wouldn't say she was against going out or having fun; she didn't see "fun" the way I did. So, she went out to do what she liked, and I did the same, but we had a good friendship. I could always talk to her. One day, I got curious about the things she liked to do and asked to go with her. I learned that she really liked live music—-almost all genres of music too. Zoë would be the girl dancing in the room when everyone else is seated. And she could dance.

Let's see…she went to the arts market and would buy stones, necklaces and bangles. She liked to people watch in the park, drink green smoothies, kayak--you know, the shit you seldom see melanated people do. But honestly, I loved all of it when I was with her. And if I hadn't gone along, I probably wouldn't know how much I could enjoy those things too. It didn't matter what she was doing; it all gave her the same level of enjoyment. Reading a book and dancing were equally exciting to her.

A part of me wondered why Zoë never asked to return the favor and come out with me some time. With my track record of coming back to the dorm and needing her to hold my braids back so they wouldn't float around the toilet in vomit, or to cover my naked ass while I puked, I understood why *no one* would ask to participate. She was her own person. And she never made me feel shitty. Never.

~

When freshman summer rolled over to fall, Zoë and I decided to move into another dorm on campus and continue rooming together. We simply kept up the lifestyle we established during first semester, but at that point, I had put most of the "out my mama house" partying behind me. I managed to escape completely failing two of the four classes I had taken the previous semester, so I was on the straight and narrow to have more success that fall. I focused on school, attended an event on campus here and there, maybe hit up a night spot once a week, and would do a few things with Zoë—if I could catch up with her.

Our fall financial aid was disbursed, and I had a little extra to spend, so I asked Zoë to head to Governor's Square with me to shop around and grab something to eat. It was always awkward to ask her to come along with me because I was the one without a car, and Zoë drove us everywhere. She had an old Camry with over 200,000 miles on it, but she loved her car—well, at least I never heard her complain about it. When it put her down, she would say, "My baby's in surgery." There were a few times over the years when her car was in line at the shop for a new timing belt, or some other "procedure" to address the noticeably shaking steering wheel, or the loud engine noise.

This trip to the mall was no different than all the others. That day, she wore a pair of yoga pants, and a shirt thin enough to see the colorful sports bra she wore underneath. Before leaving our dorm, she went for a run across campus. It was something she would do to get some air and burn energy if she had been indoors for too long, and not necessarily for weight loss, which she was far from needing. She was slender, not skinny; and had more boobs than ass, but she had one. Her skin was a little darker than normal after her run that day, and her face was dewy from perspiring.

We pulled up to the mall, and she gave me "the talk".

She said, "I don't wanna be in here all night. Let's find some shit you like, get it, and go."

"Yes, ma'am!" I responded.

Zoë hated shopping, but she always dressed well. She liked beachy attire: sundresses and shorts with various accessories. When the weather changed, she kept it simple with a sweater, some jeans, and boots or flats. Zoë didn't like shopping malls because she always found better pricing for the same shit when she patiently searched for them online. She consistently found items I'd already purchased in a store for a more reasonable price. Great finds, but they came at the expense of waiting. The need for instant gratification is constantly used to describe individuals in every generation from Millennials on, and I'm a prime example. Zoë would be amongst the small exception.

We went into Macy's, and I was struck by the display of a new line of lipsticks. The store was buzzing with young people who had a few coins to spend, so no one was at the counter to help us.

"Hellooooo," I said loudly. A few employees at a different

counter looked our way as they helped other customers, but no one came over.

"Chill out, girl," Zoë said.

"Weren't you the one who said, 'in and out'?"

"Yeah, but *your* attitude makes them come over here with *their* attitudes, and then it's all a bunch of mess. What do you want from over here anyway?"

"Lipstick. I need some fall colors now—browns, plums, maybe a deep, red color."

Zoë stared blankly at me but didn't speak.

"What?" I asked.

"You said that like I have a clue what your ass is talking about."

"Different colors go with different seasons."

"Says who?"

"Never mind. I forgot. You're such a fuckin' rebel. No rules. Trendless Tracy here." She laughed as one of the lipstick shades caught my eye. "I might like that. Grab that one for me." I pointed.

"Okay." She picked up the tester tube of plum lipstick and examined it closely.

"That one too." I pointed at a different color, and then moved down the counter for what more I could find. Zoë walked towards the opposite end.

After a minute or two, she came over to me. "This is pretty," she said.

"Let me see that." She handed over a tube of deep-red lipstick, and I read the label aloud, "*Firetruck.*" I shrugged. "I guess."

I looked at her. Zoë's face had changed. There was very little life in her eyes, which she never spared.

"What's wrong?"

"Nothing," she smirked. She reached for the lipstick from my hand. "This one reminds me of a color Daloris wore when she was in 11th grade—almost every day."

"Daloris." I had never heard her mention the name before. "Who's that?"

"My sister."

"I didn't know you had a sister."

"I know."

"It's cute. I wanna try it on," I said excitedly.

I totally missed the fact that I had learned something new about my friend, and I was so focused on buying a new lip shade, that I didn't inquire further into that sorrowful shift. In my own defense, it's also possible that Zoë didn't like to talk about it. We had been roomies for over three months, and she had finally spoken the girl's name. Plus, Zoë eventually bounced back to her normal self— at least, for a while.

"Everybody's still busy," Zoë said as she looked around. There were two tall stools in front of the counter where we stood. "Sit here. You might as well try it on while we wait. Make sure you really like it. I'll do it for you."

I must have appeared nervous to let her apply my lipstick because she grabbed the testers from my hands and said, "Look, it's lipstick, not hair bleach. If I mess it up, just wipe it off."

I sat down. "Wait," I said, and pressed my lips together. "My lips are dry. Use that moisturizer over there."

Without any sass, which I expected, she walked over for the moisturizer and came back to apply it. She pumped a single splash of the store's sanitizer into her hand and rubbed them together as she stood at my side. I parted my lips slightly, and her finger began to glide across my skin as she smoothed the moisturizer on my bottom lip, working right to left. And then she moved to my top lip, pressing here and there to saturate the area. Her breasts pressed against my arm, but she didn't notice as well as I did, or not at all.

"You don't need anything more than this." She spoke in a voice that only I could hear—being that close to her. "I like the shape of your lips. The tone is so even."

I didn't say anything. Internally, I basked in the compliment; but she touched me in a way that was so tantalizing, I found myself basking in that too.

"Alright, which color do you want first?" she asked as she looked at the assortment on the counter. "Which one do you like best? We may not have to take it off if you really like it."

"Let's do—umm—'Firetruck'."

"Okay." She grabbed the tester and a small applicator, and returned to her position, breasts against my arm.

She swept the brush gently against my lips from right to left, and I got a whiff of whatever she was wearing, mixed with perspiration from her afternoon run. The scent was subtle, but still there.

"You smell good," I said.

"Stop talking. I'm trying to put this on you. But thanks."

She dabbed a little more of the product from the tube to the brush, and from the brush to my lips. She was obviously trying to perfect them because I could feel her return to areas she had already covered.

"You know, I really like this," she said. "You definitely have the lips for it."

She handed me a mirror from the counter.

"Nice. I like it. I need a liner though." I was about to jump up and grab one, but she stopped me.

"No, just tell me which one."

I pointed. "The red one in that little cup. You do know I can do all this myself."

She came back over with the liner in hand. "Yeah, but it's been a long time since I played 'makeup' with anyone. Let me do it," she said in a voice tainted with sadness.

I admit, I started to see signals that weren't really there— her insistence to apply my lip color, her breasts against my arm, her seemingly flirtatious compliments. The wheels of my thoughts were spinning beyond control.

She positioned herself on my right side again, breasts against my arm.

"Hold still. I am not a pro at this," she said.

We were both quiet, but I could feel the warmth of her exhale against my face and, without another thought, I did it. I lifted my head, and I planted a big, red kiss on her lips.

Zoë's lips didn't linger once they had been firmly pressed against mine. It was apparent that I had kissed her, but she didn't overreact. She stood back and covered her mouth with her hands, embarrassed.

"Wow," was muffled behind her hands.

"Oh shit!" I said.

She lowered her hands and came closer to me. "I'm not a lesbian," she said in a whisper.

"Me either," I told her.

"Then what the fuck was that?"

"I had a moment," was my only explanation.

"Yeah," she chuckled. "A lesbian one. You know that's going around. I think you caught the bug." She walked away, tossed our used materials into the trash, and put the cosmetics back on the display.

I was so ashamed. Zoë had such a contagious energy that I couldn't resist an urge I had no clue was there. Zoë had already laughed it off, but I wanted to know what was going through her head. She seemed to have bounced back to her normal self.

She completed her part of the clean-up and came towards me. Her lips were covered in "Firetruck".

"I'm sorry, but I got you good," I said. "You might want to

look in the mirror."

"Yeah, I'm sure." She turned to face the mirror. She stood there, stunned—but not in a good way. It was like she had seen a ghost—or like her reflection reminded her of something that caused great despair. She stared at herself for a while before I handed her a facial wipe for her lips.

I said gently, "Nah, lipstick doesn't do those natural pouters any justice. That's coming from the lesbian rooted deep inside of me."

She laughed. "You're flirting with me, boo." She wiped her lips. "That deeply-rooted lesbian might not be as deep as you think."

After buying the tube of lipstick, we walked the mall for at least an hour—cracking jokes and acting out like we normally had. We didn't miss a beat.

It seemed Zoë had completely forgotten our encounter, but I had not. I wasn't tempted to make a second move on her, but my imagination came in handy on nights when I was alone—or shit, even when I was with someone—and I fantasized about what it would be like to explore her. I recalled nights in the old dorm where the moonlight shined over her bed, and her breasts would almost spill over her tank top while she tossed and turned on those cheap ass mattresses. I imagined crawling into bed with her, and breathing deeply as our bodies collide and our hands explored each other. We would moan until climax, and then fall asleep in all the moisture. I won't say I'm a lesbian, or bi, but my fantasies were filled with scenarios of me with other women—and mostly Zoë.

There was never an indication that Zoë considered having anything more intimate than our friendship. She was quite free sexually, but she preferred men. It didn't matter. I refused to live in my head, and was grateful that all appeared forgotten. I still had my friend. The red stain on Zoë's lips the day I kissed her lasted longer than her offense. She was quick to forgive—or was seldom offended enough to notice that someone needed to be forgiven.

~

For how long were you and Zoë roommates?

Three semesters. By the end of spring, Zoë moved into a one-bedroom duplex. She said she wanted more freedom. Zoë didn't have a lot of people over. Actually, she never had anyone over when we lived together, which is probably what made her a better roommate that most. I guess her new freedom included lighting candles and incense, which she loved but couldn't do on campus, and having a fridge large enough to stock up on all the shit she needed to make green smoothies.

Her place was comfortable, but the area was rough. It was a little off the beaten college path, and where the locals live, but it was cheap. Zoë's new, part-time job at the toy store was enough to cover it.

A raggedy garage with two doors that sat right across the street from the duplex. Zoë had no choice but to park in there since her block offered no street parking; and the property didn't have a driveway since it sat only a few meters from the street.

She made the place her own, you know, on a college student's budget. Aside from her scented candles and incense, she had deep-colored red and purple fabrics in her bedroom and on her windows. She loved throw pillows, and they were all over—-on her cheap ass couch and the floors in each room. She didn't have a TV, which she probably wouldn't have watched anyway. The only thing I hated was her thin walls. We could always hear the television of the lady next door, but Zoë made it feel good in there.

Do you think she changed after moving out on her own?

Yes. She explored the city beyond all the college life shit. Before she moved, she was constantly doing something; and after the move, she was still always on the go, but not around campus.

~

Zoë loved thrifting. From clothes to unique household items, she probably went out twice a month to find something she could treasure. I hate the smell of thrift stores, and I tend to itch whenever I walk inside one of them. To me, lurking in every thrift store is a case of scabies and crabs waiting to happen. The spread of dust mites isn't appealing, but when Zoë asked me to go out for lunch, I didn't anticipate the stop we would make at one of her favorite locations.

She would drive almost twenty miles from campus to areas where there were large, elegant homes and elaborate community parks. We assumed the city's politicians lived in those areas because the homes surrounding campus seemed occupied by blue collar workers trying to keep up with the demands of their gentrified communities. Students didn't typically venture that far for an apartment, and would be unable to afford the shit if they tried.

"This store has the good stuff," Zoë said as we hopped out of the car—her more excitedly than me.

Once we were inside, she nudged a few shirts on the rack whose colors caught her attention. As she walked towards the back of the store, she fluffed a few pillows and shuffled several handbags around. When she noticed the bright orange beach cruiser stashed underneath a hanging rug, she moved quickly for a closer look.

"Niiiiice," she said.

"It's probably broken, Zoë. Why would they get rid of it if it wasn't?"

Zoë examined the wheels and the chain of the bicycle, and then sat on its seat.

"Maybe they were moving and couldn't take it. Or they probably didn't ride it enough and it was taking up space in their garage. I don't think it's broken." She mounted the bike. "I'm gonna ride it."

"In the store?"

"Yeah. They won't let me take it outside."

I was ready to protest and convince her that we would be put out, but that didn't seem like such a bad idea, and would work in my favor. I grabbed her wallet from her hand, and she shoved off towards shelves of ceramic knickknacks, books, and dingy children's toys. She whisked through the store, circling the collection of children's clothing and shoes, and then past the men's dressing room. Store associates took notice, and one scrawny white boy attempted to get her attention, but couldn't catch her. She circled the store again; and then, stealing the boy's opportunity to confront her, she stopped at the register and jumped off. She motioned for me to come to her.

"You're getting it?" I asked her.

"Yeah. This shit is solid. You still have your bicycle, right?"

"Yes, but I don't ride it. I should drop it off here. Thrift stores pay for your things, right?"

"Nah. It's all donated."

"People gave this stuff away?"

"Yeah."

"Then hell nah. I can sell it on EBay or Craigslist or some shit, and make a few dollars."

"Keep it. You can ride with me." She pushed the bicycle forward as she was called to the register.

"You know I don't do exercise outside of walking through that damn campus."

"It's not for exercise. We can go out and get some air."

"I can get air with both feet on my balcony at home."

"One time," she said as she paid for the bicycle with a twenty-dollar bill.

"We'll see."

The following Saturday presented the perfect opportunity for the thrill-seeking Zoë. I hoped she would forget about my half-assed agreement to ride with her and just venture out on her own. After she had ridden a whole seven miles to my apartment, she was hard to deny. I grabbed my bicycle from the storage closet outside my apartment, dusted it off, and went along with her.

We were silent as we rode through various neighborhoods; I just followed Zoë's lead to wherever she was headed. After about five miles, and my regret of not bringing a bottle of water, we were on a narrow road lined with trees on each side that rebelled against the divide. They met slightly in the middle and formed a cool, canopy road that provided shade from the sun. We paddled against traffic and could see cars before they would pass us.

Zoë slowed her pace and allowed me to catch up with her.

"This is my favorite road in the city. It's even better being outside my car."

"You could have parked somewhere close and walked this road," I suggested.

"No sidewalks," she said. "It's cool. Riding through is giving me so much life."

"How long is it?"

"Maybe two-and-a-half miles."

"Well, you can go ahead. I'm tired as fuck."

"We haven't been riding long though."

"I'm thirsty. It's hot as hell out here."

"I told your ass to drink more water. Let's get to the end of the road, and then we'll stop at a corner store."

"Bet."

Zoë moved ahead of me so that we were no longer riding side-by-side. After a moment, she released the handlebars of her bicycle and extended her arms into the air as she continued to paddle the bicycle. I could see the stop sign, which signaled the road's end, and I silently celebrated.

Suddenly, an old pickup truck roared in our direction, and the driver was slow to properly align his vehicle on the roadway. I swerved quickly and came to a stop; but Zoë was caught off-guard. When she swerved, she fell completely from her bike and hurled it further into the road. I dropped my bicycle into the grass and ran over to her. She held one hand against her head, and tried to prop herself up from the ground with the other.

"Wait," I told her. "You're bleeding."

She looked at her hand and noticed the blood. She cringed. I pulled her up by her shoulders so that she sat erect from the ground. Zoë adjusted her leg and stared down at her ankle. She sobbed in pain.

"It's twisted bad," she said.

"Don't move it too much."

She cried and grabbed at her head again. "Help me, D, please."

"What can we do now? You can't ride with a twisted ankle."

"Help me, D," she said, and then passed out in the grass.

I was scared shitless by her condition, but only a few seconds after she fainted, a car passed us on the road, and then stopped. Its female driver got out and moved Zoë's bicycle closer to us, and out of the road, before she came over to assist. It took Zoë another minute to fully come to herself and sit up again.

"Do you want me to take you to a hospital?" the woman asked. "You should see a doctor."

"Yes, Zoë. You should go. You might need stiches, or something for your leg," I added.

Zoë looked at the woman's car. "Where would I put my bicycle?"

"Just leave it here, Zoë."

"No."

"You can buy another one. You only spent $20 for it."

The woman wasn't prepared to engage in our debate. "If you don't need the ride, it's fine."

"Thank you for your help, but I can manage," Zoë said.

The woman left, and Zoë grabbed her bicycle from the ground.

"You can't ride, Zoë," I told her.

"I know. I can push it home though."

She turned the bicycle around and began to walk in the opposite direction. She limped painfully, but her strides were consistent. I followed suit with my bicycle at my side.

"You can ride ahead, Destiny. You don't have to walk with me."

"I'm not leaving you out here by yourself."

It took almost three hours to get to Zoë's place on her injured ankle, and with the bicycles in tow, but we made it.

~

Zoë seemed quite stubborn. Would you agree?

She invented stubborn. If her mind was set on something, she wouldn't give--not even a little. It makes better sense now. I guess it is easier to be single if you're as stubborn as Zoë was; then you wouldn't be concerned about things not going your way, or having to compromise to spare other people's feelings. Zoë didn't compromise, or make excuses, for how she was wired.

This may seem random but, since you two were close friends, what would you say was Zoë's superpower?

That's easy. Her ability to not give a fuck. She wrote the manual on it. And not like the loud chicks we see in the club who's ready to swing at a bitch for looking at her funny, or the ones starting shit on Instagram--not that kind of "not giving a fuck". Zoë was quiet about it. She was unmovable. And it wasn't for some grand purpose. Her superpower simply enabled her to *be*.

What was Zoë's relationship with her family like?

Umm… She never talked about her family. I met her foster mom when school started, but that was it. I asked her how she wound up in foster care, and she told me that her mom died when she was little. She didn't say how, so I figured she didn't want to talk about it. Death is a touchy subject for some people. I can't imagine what I would do if I lost my mom.

What about her dating life? You mentioned Zoë was better off being single.

I must be honest. Zoë and I *said* we were best friends since freshman summer. We never were. Zoë was *my* best friend. I wasn't hers. When it came to dating, I went through a long, rough patch to figure all this shit out. She was always there to listen, and had a way of getting me to think. She wouldn't outright say that I was wrong, or being dumb as fuck.

The night I keyed my ex-boyfriend's car because he wouldn't answer my phone calls, I vented to Zoë. Before I caught a ride over there, all she asked was: "Will you feel better when you're done? Will it change your situation with him?" I knew I would still be angry after I keyed his shit, and he would still be a jackass when I was finished, but I still thought it would help. It didn't. I was still mad, and dude thought I was crazy and stopped messing with me altogether.

But I wasn't Zoë's best friend. When I think

back, I don't remember shutting up long
enough for her to talk in depth about much
of anything. There were a few guys that I
knew of, but I can't say if she had any issues
with them. Either she didn't have any, or
just didn't tell me about it.

**What do you know about her relationship with
Marcus?**

Not much. I know they used to hang out a lot.
He's a baller, but Zoë wasn't a groupie. I
don't think she went to any games at all
while she was here, but I believe she really
liked Marcus. She had nothing but good things
to say, but that was Zoë. She only wanted to
talk about the good in people. She said that
if she did, she could experience more of it.

**What were some of the good things she
mentioned about Marcus?**

She liked how he made himself available to
her. Don't get me wrong; he didn't crawl
behind her, or grovel at her feet. She liked
how hard he tried to understand her, and
would even test her at times. With Zoë, that
couldn't have been easy. She was quite
complex.

What made her so hard to understand?

That's the thing. Nothing about her was hard
to understand. She was beyond unique, and
wasn't what we'd call "normal". The fact that
she didn't give a fraction of a fuck about
who understood her made her more intriguing.
I guess that's what lured Marcus in. He
tried, and she was grateful for that.

71

Did she ever talk about sex?

She liked her privacy, so I never got any details; but she wasn't celibate. She told me she enjoyed sex. I know for a fact that she loved her *own* pussy.

What?

She had these little noni rituals she would do at least twice a month. While her coochie wasn't completely off-limits to the guys, it was still sacred to her. Who the hell knew the criteria for her to give it up to one person and not another.

Did Zoë ever mention how things ended with Marcus?

Umm…not exactly. I asked about him one day after they stopped hanging out. All she said was that she wasn't enough for him. Not that she didn't feel worthy of *him*, but he couldn't be satisfied with what she was willing to give.

Do you think Zoë's "break-up" with Marcus had anything to do with what happened to her?

Oh, hell no. Marcus was—-let's see-—spring and summer '17. Zoë was far removed from that relationship when she died. She met someone else that fall—-Travis.

What can you tell me about him?

Not much. I didn't even know about the guy until Zoë found herself in a situation.

~

It was late February, or early March, of 2018. After I returned to school from winter break, Zoë and I had only seen each other once or twice, and that wasn't like us. We usually found a chance to get together once a week. I knew her classes had become more demanding, and so were mine, but I missed my friend, and I wanted to see her.

When I called, she said she was at a popular coffee shop not too far from campus. It's a place where students go to hang out, and especially to gather and study for finals at all hours of the night. The place never closes. One time, Zoë and I were there until sunrise. The library was packed, and staying in the dorm meant saying, "Fuck it," and falling asleep. She drilled me for hours at the coffee shop to help me on a history exam. I left the spot and went straight to class—no toothbrush or breath mints—but I passed.

When I walked into the coffee shop that evening, there were only three other patrons. Zoë sat near the back where the lights were low, reading a book and sipping from a mug. She smiled when she noticed me, and put her book on the table.

"Hey love!" I said.

"I thought you would be here an hour ago."

"I was stalling. I thought you would leave here so we could find a better spot to eat. I am hungry, and the lil' refreshments they have here is not gonna do it."

"We can go somewhere else if you're hungry," she suggested.

"You look comfortable and shit. All that's missing is the dusty, yellow blanket you had back at the dorm." She chuckled. "I won't make you leave."

"I'm good. Just been real chill today. Wish I knew what happened to that blanket though—while you're playing."

"Someone mistook it for an old rug and tossed it. It was so raggedy and stiff." I took off my jacket. "How long you been here?"

"Umm—maybe 6 or 7 hours."

"What? Why the hell you been here so long?"

"I met a guy friend here around 1 o'clock. When he left, I got into this book. At the end of every chapter I try to leave, but then I push it one more chapter, and then another. I'm damn near finished now."

"At least you're productive. So, what's been up? Who's this guy friend?" I leaned in.

"Just a guy."

"Cute? FAMU? FSU? Greek?" I wanted details.

"Yes, cute. And neither."

"Y'all hooking up, or he's something serious?"

"Neither. He was a good guy, but we agreed to just be cool."

"You alright?" I didn't ask because her emotions resembled that of a girl who had just experienced a break-up. I asked because I thought it was the thing to do in moments like those.

"I'm good. Why have you been M.I.A.? What's going on with you?" Zoë asked.

For an hour, I told her about Dwayne, the guy whose Beamer was repossessed while we were riding in it; and Shawn, who I met back home but didn't want to fuck with anymore because he had a small dick; and about the money I lent to a friend who posted on Instagram about her new red bottoms, but the bitch owed me $200; and about how classes were kicking my ass but I was eager to hit senior status. Zoë sat there and listened. She looked me in the eyes, and soaked up every word of it.

One of the baristas came over to ask if we needed anything.

I placed an order. "A caramel macchiato for each of us, please. Make hers nondairy." It was one of our favorite things.

"No. No, thank you. Another ginger tea, please."

"Whaaaaat? You? Isn't it the reason you started coming here in the first place? Theirs isn't the best anymore?"

"No. Pregnant women can't have caffeine, and their decaf sucks."

I was shocked by her response.

"You're pregnant, Zoë?"

"Facts," she said with a smile.

"When did you find out? By who? Why you ain't tell me?"

"I just found out a few days ago. It's not *your* baby, so why would I call you without telling him first?"

"Tell who?" I asked.

"The guy I said I met here earlier."

"But I thought you said you guys ended it."

"Yep."

"You gotta give me more than one word on that one, Zoë."

"He decided to fix things with his wife."

"What—the—fuck. He's married. How old is this dude?"

"He's 28. And I knew he was separated when we started hanging out last year, so it's not a big deal that he decided to make it work with her."

"And what did he say about the baby?"

The barista walked our drinks over and placed them on the

table. Zoë slowly pressed her lips to the ceramic mug and took a small sip of the piping hot tea.

"I didn't tell him," she said.

"Why? You got the guy here, and you didn't tell him?"

"No. The man has a whole life. He told me his news before I could tell him mine. And when I thought about it, I figured he would be better off focusing on his relationship."

"But your ass is giving him a whole fuckin' baby?"

"I'm not *giving* him anything. Just taking it one day at a time."

"Ohh, okay. I get it. You're not gonna keep it."

"That's not it. I am. I'll sleep on it tonight and see what tomorrow brings."

"Girl, this shit is big—finishing school, having a baby—but you're sipping tea and acting like you're deciding between a Coke or Pepsi."

"Everything is as big as I make it."

That was it. She didn't say a word against the guy who abandoned her and the baby for his wife, nor did she seem discouraged or hurt by the situation. She was more mellow than normal that evening, but I could credit that to the dim lighting and ginger teas. I was more disappointed by the situation than Zoë expressed. She was only a few credits shy of being a senior when she discovered she was pregnant. It would be our final year together, and our last opportunity to live our best life before truly "adulting".

The tides turned quickly, and I found myself in Zoë's shoes. I was pregnant by a boyfriend I had dated off and on for a number of years since high school. Zoë was about seven months along in her pregnancy at that point but, as always, she was a listening ear. Unlike Zoë, my only option was to get rid of it.

She never judged my decision to go through with the procedure, or tried to convince me to change my mind. Instead, she offered to come along so I wouldn't go through it by myself. We drove three hours to the closest facility that still offered abortions, and she stopped twice to pee. I couldn't imagine what it was like for her to sit in the waiting area of an abortion clinic, plump and pregnant, while I was in the back wiping my slate clean and preparing to move on with life.

After the procedure, and the long, quiet drive back, she took me to my apartment and came inside for a while. She wanted to wait until I showered and was ready for bed before she left.

I stepped out of the bathroom with a fresh maxi pad wedged between my thighs and wearing a long polka dot nightgown my mother had given me for Christmas, and went into the kitchen for a snack.

"You want some ice cream?" I offered.

"I can't have that."

"What you mean? Don't all pregnant women like ice cream?"

"Dairy would give this one *extreme* gas."

"Shit. Since you put emphasis on 'extreme', maybe not today."

"Maybe never. I don't do dairy, remember?" She chuckled to herself. "The almond milk and coconut milk I used to buy would take up damn near half of my fridge space when we lived in the dorm."

"Yeah, that's right."

"Nothing's changed."

I looked at her belly. "That's a damn lie, Wobble Queen."

I piled the bowl high with strawberry ice cream, and we went into my bedroom. I hated having company in the common areas because my roommates were all nosey and rude as fuck.

Zoë used a pillow to prop herself up on the bed while I sat at my desk to devour the ice cream. She must have been tired because, within minutes, she had shut her eyes. Instantly, a thought occurred to me that I believed was genius, and I wanted to share it.

"Zoë. You up?"

"Yeah. Resting my eyes."

"Listen to this. What if women were closed for business?"

She said, sleepily, "Isn't the saying, 'open for business'?"

"Exactly, but not all business is good business. Sometimes we need to make an executive decision to close the fuckin' doors. Taking care of our personal business first is everything," I spoke passionately.

"Yeah, I like that," she said.

"Yep." I was excited. I started to pace the room with the bowl of ice cream in my hands. "Closed for business—these degrees, these coins, this whole life I'm about to get. I saw that Netflix series about sex—the one with Janelle Monáe's voice narrating the episodes. It said men used to take birth control, but their soft asses couldn't handle the side effects. But *we* have to take the shit to not end up in the damn clinic? Oh, hell no!"

I was preaching good to a congregation that was unable to partake in excitement created by my newfound freedom. Zoë, whose unborn baby boy caused her belly to bulge over her lap, sat and watched me.

"I think I'll get a shirt made in every color too."

"A walking billboard for no sex, huh?"

"Damn right! These niggas got women out here dealing with their mess, and nobody looks like a damn fool but us."

Zoë didn't say anything, and I couldn't read her face.

I turned my excitement down a few notches, and placed the bowl of ice cream on the night stand before I climbed into bed next to her. "That's not how I wanted that to come out. I didn't mean that *you're* a fool. I'm just saying…"

"I know what you meant."

"But are you okay?" I asked.

"Yeah, it makes no sense to have regrets. It won't change anything."

I put my head on her chest, and she gently massaged my scalp.

"I don't know how you do it." I told her. "And be so chill about everything."

"One day at a time," she said.

~

So, did Zoë ultimately have the baby?

Yes, she did. I don't think she considered any other option. She wasn't obsessed, but she owned a few baby books, went to her appointments faithfully, and started to pick up things here and there for the baby. I asked if she wanted a baby shower, but she didn't.

Why not? Do you believe she was ashamed?

No. Only people who care what others think of them is ever ashamed. Zoë did everything she was supposed to do as a woman expecting a baby. I don't think her refusal to have the shower stemmed from negative feelings about the baby or her choices. It's possible that Zoë wouldn't even know who to invite to something like that. As her closest friend, I can say assuredly that I was more than likely her *only* friend. Zoë was a very private girl. She participated in events and was involved on campus, but she kept almost everyone she connected with right where she met them--on campus.

Were you there when she went into labor or delivered the baby?

No. I was in Tampa with family when Zoë was in the hospital. She called once they were released and told me she was okay. She never shared details about it. Based on my experience with Zoë, that either meant it was really painful, or didn't go well for her. She always avoided conversations along those lines. She was okay, and that's what mattered, so I didn't mind her sparing the details.

So, who has the baby? The father?

No one told you?

Told me what? It wasn't until now that I learned Zoë even had a baby. Where is he now?

He died. Zoë took him with her.

INTERVIEW FOUR

Date: Wednesday, January 15, 2020
Time: 9:04 AM
Location: Tallahassee, Florida

SOURCE: TRAVIS DOBSON

It was a Tuesday night in August of 2017. A colleague and I decided to go out for some wings at a local sports bar after putting out a few fires at the Senate office. We sat down, ordered our food and a few beers, and we spoke between glances at the television screens mounted high on the walls. When she walked in, I first noticed her hair—big natural curls pulled back from a face that would cause anyone to look twice.

I watched as she spoke to the hostess and then held up a single finger, perhaps to indicate she was a party of one. I wanted a closer look at her, and hoped she would be escorted to my area where there were two empty tables. She was. The way the tables aligned, she and I were seemingly sitting next to each other—just at different tables. One of the mounted screens that had my attention was right above her head, so it enabled me to steal glances of her as she ordered her food, or sipped from her glass. She noticed as I looked in her direction, and flashed me a half-smile before turning away.

"Good evening," I said.

"Good evening," she responded.

79

"I'm looking at that screen over there."

She turned to see the screen I pointed to, and then back to me.

"I know." She smiled again.

"As long as it doesn't bother you…"

"It doesn't bother me now, but when my food comes it might. I don't think I'll be able to tell if you're watching me graze or the football game above my head."

I chuckled. "I'll watch something else once you get your food then. I'm Travis. What's your name?" I stood to shake her hand.

"Zoë."

I sat back down. My colleague, whose back had been turned to her, spun around and took notice, and then flashed me the raised, "damn bro" brow.

"You waiting for friends?"

"No. It's just me. Today is my birthday."

"And you don't have friends coming out with you?"

"I'd rather spend it alone. I'm not big on celebrations."

"Obviously, you're still under 21, otherwise you would have a drink in your hand."

"Partly true. I'm 20, but this time next year I'll still be enjoying a refreshing Arnold Palmer," she said, and gestured as though she were in a television commercial. "I don't drink. Unless you count kombucha. That shit is like cat nip for me."

I laughed. "Cat nip? Really? I guess if you've always been sober, kombucha would feel like you've smoked some herb. But how do you know you don't drink if you're not old enough to do it yet?"

"It's frowned upon, but everyone is old enough to drink— just not in public. I don't drink in private either."

"Why? If you don't me asking."

"I've seen what it can do to people."

Her smile dimmed, and she took a sip from her glass.

"What are your plans after this?"

"I'm going out for a cupcake."

"A cupcake."

"Yeah. It's like a ritual."

"No parties? Movies? Date?"

"Nah. School night. I have to be up by 7."

I contemplated a moment, not wanting to be too forward or infringe upon her solo birthday ritual, but I didn't want to walk away and never see her again.

"Do you mind if I take you out for that cupcake?"

She looked at me with a countenance that was ready to say *no,* but it softened.

"There's a bakery on Monroe. It's open late. Enjoy the evening with your friend. When you're done, if you feel like coming through, I'll be there until 11."

I wanted a phone number, but I couldn't ask for more; permitting me to meet her that evening was already a compromise.

The waitress brought our food to the table, so I ate and engaged in conversation with my tablemate. I can't say what she ordered, but it was small. She ate and, at some point, got up to leave. I caught a small glimpse of her exit, but I was confident I would see her again that night. I was in complete control of that.

It was well after ten. Once I finished eating, I quickly parted ways with my colleague and hopped into my car. The bakery was only six minutes away.

There were at least eight patrons in the well-lit cupcake shop that night. Zoë sat alone at a table near the front window, and I could see her as I pulled into the parking lot.

When I walked in, she was reading a book. The cupcake she'd ordered sat on the table in front of her.

"What you reading?" I said as I slid into the chair.

"A Pam Grout book," she said.

"For class?"

"No." She placed the book on the table.

"What did you get?"

She tapped the top of the box with her fingers. "Strawberry."

"Your favorite?"

She shrugged. "You can say that."

It was time to be forward.

"Are you with someone?"

"You," she responded with eyes focused on me.

I blushed inwardly. "I meant—are you in a relationship?"

"Oh those? No."

"What do you mean *those*?"

"I don't know." She backed down from my question. "But no, I'm not in a relationship."

I thought it would be the perfect opportunity for her to reciprocate and ask if I was seeing anyone, but she didn't.

"Are you ordering a cupcake? Red velvet is the shit, but the classic is good too if you're not trying to be fancy."

"Nah. I'm good. Still full from that plate of wings."

She picked up the cupcake, opened the box, and made it pretend-float in the air. "You don't know what you're missing," she said as the fragrant cupcake passed my nose.

"Maybe I'll get one for later."

She closed the box. "Thought so."

"You wanna come over here with me since you're the cupcake expert?"

She stood, and we walked to the counter together. The girl who worked the register that night must have been ready to get off because her attitude was beyond shitty. When I approached, there were no pleasantries—a "good evening" or "welcome in". She stood behind the register, rolled her eyes a few times, and looked at us as if to say, "What you want?" without opening her mouth at all. Zoë looked at the assortment of sweets behind the glass and hadn't paid the cashier any attention.

I moved close to her, and only spoke loud enough for her to hear me. "You see this?"

"What?" she said.

"What's up with the girl at the register?"

She glanced in the cashier's direction. "I don't know her," she responded, and continued to look through the glass.

"No—I mean—her attitude."

"The more attention you give it, the worse it will get," she said, and then pointed out a few cupcakes. "If you're into chocolate, that one is amazing."

"Yeah, maybe I'll try a chocolate and a red velvet."

I walked over to the cashier whose annoyance had nothing to do with me. "I would like red vel—."

"How many?" she cut me off.

I was the recipient of some undeserved energy, and was prepared to walk away. "Hold that thought," I said, and went back over to Zoë.

"Don't think I'm being cheap, but I don't spend money in places that don't treat me like I'm spending money. I don't think I want anything."

Zoë looked over my shoulder at the girl, and then back to me. "Like I said, we don't know her. It's fine if you don't buy anything, but that girl doesn't own this place. She just works here. You'll penalize the owner, not her. Write a review or talk to management before you decide if it's a place you'll return to," she happily suggested. "Do you want cupcakes?"

"Sure," I said.

"Then let's get them." She smiled and moved towards the

register.

The cashier looked at Zoë with the same mug.

"Hey again," Zoë said with great vibrancy. "Do you mind getting some cupcakes for us, please?"

"What would you like?" she asked—her eyes, widened.

"One chocolate, and one red velvet," Zoë said in a joyful tone—possibly too joyful for that hour.

The cashier pressed the screen a few times. "That'll be $7.46."

Zoë slid out of the way, and I stepped up to use my card. I got another glimpse of the girl. Her energy had shifted—only slightly, but noticeably. After the payment processed, she boxed up my selections, and handed them over with a "Have a good night." We went back to our seats.

"I guess she was alright," I said to Zoë.

"People are exactly who you expect them to be. You expect someone to treat you poorly, and they will. Expect bad service, and you'll get it. One woman can have a relationship with a guy, and say he was horrible in their relationship. That same guy could move on to a new situation, and his partner could totally adore him. It's likely he didn't change at all, and some would assume his new lady had settled. His new partner simply *chose* to see the good in him, and in return, he churned out more 'good'."

"I hear you, but I didn't expect to receive that kind of attitude."

"No, but you were trying to read her. You assumed she had a bad attitude by watching her face. By the time you got to the register, you unknowingly expected to experience bad attitude, and you did."

"Mm hm. So, what's your strategy."

"Always expect the best from everyone. Try to see something good. And if that fails, smile. It's a challenge to be hard-faced if someone is smiling at you."

"Try to see the good, huh." I pondered a moment. "It's getting late, but I want to see you again."

"And you want my number?" she asked.

"No. I mean—yes—but I have to tell you something first."

She shifted her head towards the opposite shoulder and listened.

I chuckled nervously. "I've never had to do this. I was—am—married." I thought about lying, or never having this conversation with her, but I couldn't. I would rather chance it with the truth. "She left six months ago, but we're still married, and we talk."

"I understand," was all Zoë said.

"Okay." I couldn't think of how to follow-up Zoë's non-inquisitive response.

"I have to go, but take my number," she said.

I didn't see or hear from her in the days surrounding the night we met, although I had sent her a text or two and called one afternoon. I thought my confession scared her away, but after a week and a half, she sent a text that said, "Hope you're well." I replied, but that message also went unanswered. There was no effort put into developing anything more than what was—an occasional text—until the storm came.

Hurricane Irma shut down the city for days as meteorologists anticipated damaging winds and flooding. I was at home when I received a text from Zoë who said she was just checking on me. To my surprise, when I replied, so did she. I wanted to keep the momentum going, so suggested that we not be alone in the storm. She agreed and invited me over for brunch at her apartment.

I didn't waste a minute. I showered, dressed, and was out the door within the hour. When I entered her address into my cell phone's GPS, her place was only 20 minutes away from mine in normal traffic, but the roadways were clear because of the impending hurricane, so I knew I would arrive sooner.

The wind was strong enough to shove at my car when it picked up speed. The trees swayed violently. When I pulled up to her place, it was almost one o'clock in the afternoon. There was nowhere to park on her street, so I walked almost three blocks in harsh wind that made tiny droplets of rain sting when they hit my face. I could feel my sweatpants and t-shirt become wetter with each step I took.

Zoë's place was in a small, cream-colored duplex in an old neighborhood that hadn't been touched by gentrification. I was about to knock, but stopped short when the adjacent door opened instead. It was Zoë. She signaled for me to hurry in from the rain.

"Ah man," she said. "You're soaked."

"I didn't know I would have to park in the next town to come here," I said as I examined my clothes.

"Forgot to mention that. My bad."

I looked at her. "I would hug you, but—."

"It's cool. You'll dry eventually. I don't have another shirt for you, but I can grab a towel. Let me get it."

She walked into the other room, and I observed her

apartment. She had a small couch, and tons of pillows all over the floor. There was a television stand at the front of the room near the windows, but no television. Instead, she had a record player, and a mellow jazz tune played. The room smelled sweet.

I checked the back of my gear, which was fairly dry, and decided to take a seat on the couch. Zoë returned with the towel, and I dried my arms and face. She sat next to me, and brought her legs up to sit Indian-style, which was a challenge in her fitted jeans.

We sat and talked for at least an hour, but neither of us looked at the time. The winds started to pick up, and the walls of her home rattled. They were so thin, I swear you could feel the moisture from the rainfall outside.

"Hey. You got me distracted. What happened to brunch?" I asked.

"That's right. I *did* say that." She visibly clenched her teeth.

"What? You don't have anything in there to eat? Everything is closed. It would be almost impossible to get something right now."

"I do. I do." She started to get up.

The walls rattled again, and then there was an exploding sound. The record player stopped.

"What was that?" she asked.

"Let me check it out." I went to the window and noticed a transformer emitting white and blue light. "It looks like a transformer's blown. No power, I'm sure."

"Wow. And I was ready to make you a huge—what time is it? Lunch." She snapped her fingers jokingly and smiled. At her kitchen pantry, she pulled two unopened boxes from the shelf. "Frosted Flakes or Apple Jacks? Non-generic too."

"Apple Jacks." I joined her at the counter as she filled two bowls with cereal. She poured in the milk before returning the carton to her fridge, and I noticed what was inside.

"At least the milk won't be wasted," she said.

"You weren't planning to make brunch today, were you?" I inquired.

"What makes you say that?" We both took in a spoonful of cereal from our bowls.

"Your fridge is bare," I crunched. "I don't know what you can make from almond milk, baking soda, and leftover takeout."

"You would be surprised." She chewed her cereal.

"Be serious. You weren't planning to cook."

"What I'm prepared for and what I plan are sometimes on two different wavelengths. It seems that everything always works itself out." She shrugged and shoved another spoonful of cereal into her mouth.

"You're without power, and the one thing you have to eat in here doesn't require any. Seems careless, but I guess you can say it worked itself out."

"And you're a psychopath if you don't think a midday bowl of cereal is a feast," she added.

After cereal, she lit a few candles as we started to lose the sunlight through the windows. She pulled out her cell phone and began to play Esperanza Spalding's *Junjo* album.

"Hey, I'm definitely a fan, but you might want to save your battery in case of an emergency, or if someone tries to reach you."

She placed her phone on the TV-less stand and plopped down next to me.

"Let's see. There's plenty of rain outside for water. Enough cereal for maybe 2-3 more days if we ration ourselves two bowls each day. And there is no one more important at this moment than the one who is here with me right now."

The woman had a way of making a man feel like he was the most important thing in the world one moment, and then question if she ever existed in the next. Zoë wasn't imagined, but real. And when I was with her, the attention and focus on me was damn near unbearable. When I spoke, she listened. And if she had a thought amid my speaking, she seemed to make a mental note and would return to it after I'd said my part. Even if the conversation bounced from topic to topic and an hour had passed, she remembered. Our eyes connected for just long enough. She would make the right gesture—a head nod, or a slight sound, or a smirk—at the right moment to indicate that she had heard me. Or she would tighten her forehead when dissecting complex ideas. I studied her. When she spoke, she never elevated her voice. The things that excited her yielded a smile or laughter, but her speaking voice was quite sultry.

She spoke of her favorites pastimes and adventures with her best friend. She mentioned poetry the kids in juvie would recite to her to prove that her time with them was not in vain.

"But I think they're actually proving they need *more* time with me. A few tweaks, and maybe they won't nominate the guy who managed to rhyme 'piss' with 'diss' for the 'Best Poem' award."

"That bad, huh?"

She chuckled and gently placed her hand over her face.

"I like that," I said.

"What?" She continued to laugh. "It shouldn't be this damn funny."

"It's okay to admit that someone completely sucks at something."

She burst into laughter.

"But that's not what I meant," I continued.

"What?" she asked again.

"That—your laughter."

"What about it?" She calmed herself.

"I don't know how to describe it. It's like you've had it bottled up for a while, and only recently released it."

"Huh?" she said.

"You ever meet a man on his first day outside of prison?"

"No, but I can imagine."

"That's what your laughter feels like—free."

Her laughter came to a complete close.

"You noticed my laugh—my smile. So, you've been watching my lips, huh?"

"They *are* attached to your face, and I can't help but notice them."

"You could stare directly at my forehead." She slapped her forehead playfully.

"That would be creepy as hell."

"Maybe, but at least I would know you're not plotting ways to kiss me." We locked eyes, and kept them there. "Or, imagining how soft they would feel against yours," she said.

Our faces moved closer together, and I leaned in and kissed her. Our lips parted and our tongues met for the first time. Zoë gripped the side of my t-shirt and pulled me closer—so close that I was basically on top of her, locked in a kiss. After a moment, she pressed her hands firmly against my chest and I sat up, puzzled.

She faced me as she stood from the couch and unbuttoned her pants, lowered the zipper, and then pulled them down past the black thongs she wore. She lost her balance, but caught it by grabbing the edge of the couch. With her pants at her knees, I noticed a scar on the back of her right thigh. It was dark brown in color, and extended completely from one side to the other.

"What happened there?" I asked her.

She rubbed her hand along the back of her thigh, and gripped the scar firmly with her hand. "I had an accident when I was a kid."

She shifted her body so that I could no longer see it, pressed her knee into the couch and removed her pants from around her feet. She crawled on top of me and kissed my neck. To the mix of Esperanza's voice, howling wind and rustling leaves, in candlelight and the scent of lavender, and all over the pillowed floor, Zoë and I made love.

~

What were things like between you and Zoë after the storm?

Back to how they were after the bakery. I would call or text, and she wouldn't respond for days, if she did at all. Although she seemed genuine when she told me there wasn't anyone else in the picture, the fact that I couldn't connect with her when I wanted to, made me think otherwise.

How often were you two able to connect?

We saw each other at least ten times between October and December. We always met on her terms—when she wanted and always at her place. She liked to be in control. Only once did she permit me to take her to dinner. I had moments when I thought she didn't want to be seen in public with me. But again, I couldn't imagine she would be dishonest. She had no reason to be. I had my own situation.

Speaking of your situation, did Zoë ever express how she felt about you being married after you began your sexual relationship?

Zoë and I had plenty of pillow talk, usually after sex, since we didn't connect otherwise. I know it's in poor taste to discuss past relationships when you're with someone new, but the situation with my wife wasn't fully resolved, and I found myself explaining it to Zoë.

How exactly did you explain it?

I told her how my wife and I married three years earlier while I was trying to solidify some opportunities in politics. I was a focused man, but not on her or our marriage. I can count on one hand the number of dates I'd taken her on, and the number of nights I fell asleep in bed next to her. I guess she didn't sign up to be a single-married woman, and it weighed on her. She wanted to call it off. At the time, I couldn't manage my career and a possible divorce. Plus, I truly loved her. So, I asked her to take some time away from our marriage. If she still wanted a divorce after a few months apart, I would go through with it. I needed a level of patience and support from her that she couldn't give me; and there were many things that I was unable to give her as well.

When I explained it to Zoë, she understood. It was unexpected, but nothing about Zoë was predictable. She was easy to be with—-didn't ask for anything. And although not getting a response from her annoyed the hell out of me, I appreciated the lack of clinginess, or overwhelming need for me. I was still very focused on progressing in my career. Some mornings, I would apologize for leaving abruptly, and her only response was always to "follow bliss", and she would smile. You see, we worked on many levels, but we ended things after a couple of months.

Why did the relationship end between you and Zoë?

I decided to work towards a better relationship with my wife. What I had with Zoë was so inconsistent and unpredictable that I can't even call it a relationship.

~

The holidays rolled around, and things began to slow down at the office. I spent more time in my home office than I had all year. It had been at least a week since I'd heard from Zoë when I received a text message a few days before Christmas.

"How are you spending the holidays?" it read.

I responded, "With you."

I didn't expect a response, or for her to take my firm suggestion seriously, but she did.

"Then why aren't you here?" she responded.

"I haven't been able to find the four calling birds."

"What?" She typed.

"The 12 days of Christmas…"

"Ha ha! Cute. You might want to know that it's not a countdown *to* Christmas, but a count that starts *on* Christmas."

"Oh really? I guess I never cared enough to get the facts straight."

"Forgive yourself," she messaged. "And I'll take a four-pack of candles instead."

We made plans for me to come over that evening. Although it was the latter half of December, the weather was mild, and it felt good outdoors. My intent was to take her out for dinner at one of my favorite restaurants, which has a great patio and those tall, heating lamps that helps its patrons keep warm when it's chilly outside. I text her to be dressed to leave for dinner by 7 p.m., but first, I wanted to stop and pick up the requested candles so that I wouldn't arrive emptyhanded.

I pulled up to the shopping mall and rushed into a Yankee Candle store. I grabbed vanilla, apple, and lavender fragrances, and a large jar of MidSummer's Night—a personal favorite.

I was running behind by at least fifteen minutes, but it could guarantee Zoë would be completely dressed and ready to go by the time I got there. I knocked on the door, and waited a minute or so before she answered. She was far from ready, but I couldn't complain.

Zoë was completely naked, and she held the door wide open. The lights of the burning candles in her apartment flickered when the air entered from outside. A wisp of cool breeze brushed across her bare skin, and she shivered. I stepped inside with the candles in tow, and blocked the view of her nakedness from the road.

"What are you doing?" I asked.

"I'm hungry," she said as I closed the door and locked it.

"Okay. That's why I said to get dressed."

"Not for food," she responded, and then she wrapped both of her arms around my neck, pressed her nude body against mine, and kissed me.

It was hard—literally—but after a moment, I separated from her lips long enough to ask if she was sure she didn't want to go out. She leaned closer, and we were locked in a kiss again. Her hand caressed my arm and she grabbed the bag of candles. She dropped them on top of a pillow on the floor without breaking the kiss, and then pulled me into the direction of her bedroom. We stayed there—for three days.

I could have left, but the alternative was to return to a quiet house without my wife, and with whom I had shared many previous Christmas holidays. Besides, it felt good to be there with Zoë. There wasn't a television, so we busied ourselves with card games, Scrabble or Monopoly, between sex and getting dressed enough to answer the door for food deliveries—Chinese stir fry, some Cuban dishes, or rice and peas, and plantains from a Jamaican spot. Zoë never said she was vegan, but I noticed that what she desired to eat always aligned with the diet. It was the laziest three days of my entire adult life, and no one expected an apology for it.

On our third day together, Zoë and I were engaged in a competitive game of Scrabble. We were on each other's tails in points, and we both only had three pieces remaining. The bag of letters had long been emptied.

"L-O-C-K-I-T," Zoë spelled aloud.

"Whatever. Go ahead and take that off," I said.

"What?" she asked innocently.

"I know you know better than that. It's spelled with an 'e', not an 'i', Zoë."

"Says who?"

"This isn't even an argument. Stop trying to cheat."

"I'm not. It's a new addition to the dictionary."

"Yeah? Which one?"

"Urban. It describes one who desires to keep someone for themselves. They 'lockit' down," she said convincingly.

I laughed. "Well, we're not using the urban dictionary this game. If we were, I would have added this T-Y to 'lit' three rounds ago."

"Damn," she said, and lifted the pieces from the board just

a little. "You sure?" she asked.

I gave her a head nod, and she placed the letter tiles back onto the holder. She searched the board for other places to use her final pieces.

"How you feel about that though?" I asked.

"About what?" Her eyes wandered the board.

"Being locked down. Relationships. Marriage."

"I don't know. I don't think about them."

"Why not? Everybody does."

"Well, that statement isn't true if I just said I don't."

"Why would you be an exception?"

"Would any exception know why it is one? It just is. I don't see myself as an exception—maybe 'exceptional'. If that's what you're reaching for, I'll take it." She smirked, and shuffled her tiles around on the wooden holder for the fiftieth time.

"I wasn't."

She looked directly at me. "What do you want me to say? My heart has been broken? I don't believe in marriage? I'm a commitment-phobe? I'm anti-relationships? I'm secretly a lesbian?"

I shrugged.

She continued, "None of those things would be true. I honestly just don't know."

"I remember high school, and especially undergrad. Girls were ready to land a guy who could be their 'sweetheart', and who would marry them someday."

"That's cool," she responded as she checked the score sheet.

"You didn't have a high school sweetheart?"

"No."

"Why not? You're a pretty girl. You're smart as hell, and you take good care of yourself."

"Don't forget—my coochie's good too."

"Umm—it's alright," I said playfully. She picked up a pillow from the floor and threw it at my face. I swat it down and it collided with the Scrabble board—shifting all the pieces out of place.

"See. You play too much," I said.

"Whelp! That's game. I win!"

"I knew you would find a way to cheat."

"You make it so easy," she said, and began to collect the pieces. They trickled into the bag. "Why do you come around, Travis? What do you like about me?"

I thought about it. "You're nice, passionate, a great listener. You know how to have fun and enjoy the moment."

"Isn't that enough for a woman to give to a man?"

"What if he wants something deeper—a commitment?"

"No. He wants ownership. I'm not against the idea if that's what people choose to do, but I don't want to be possessed by anyone."

"Marriage doesn't mean that a man owns his woman, or vice versa."

"Okay, maybe 'own' is not the right word. 'Control' might be a better one. At some point, I may be open to having someone dictate what I do with my life or how I spend my days, but that day is not today." She folded the board and placed it back into the box.

"He doesn't control her either though."

"I guess you're right. That would explain why your wife isn't with you." She looked at me immediately after her mouth released the comment. "That was insensitive," she said.

"No. You're right. I couldn't control whether she would stay or go. It was her choice."

"I don't know her, but if every married person is presented with the choice to stay or go, wouldn't you feel better knowing that a woman would more than likely choose to stay? All I'm saying is, I don't believe I could be that person right now, and I own that shit. It seems like most guys would prefer a lie—for me to say I desire something I don't. Lying to you means lying to myself—and it's no different from the way you and your wife lie to each other."

"There haven't been any lies between us. I'm nothing but honest with her."

"Every time you said you loved each other was a lie. You loved what it felt like to have her around; and she did the same. When you weren't there, she walked away. It wasn't the man she loved, but what she felt when she had the man in the way she wanted him. And you know why you let her leave? Because she didn't make you feel supported in the way you needed either. It's quite self-serving. I can't believe that's love."

"None of the guys you've been with ever say they love you?"

"If they did, I didn't believe them."

"Why? Do you think they were lying?"

"No. I think they said what they believed they felt at the time—but I knew they didn't fully know what it meant."

"How could you know for sure? There are many men who are tapped into their emotions."

"Love isn't an emotion. I could tell because somewhere down the line they would express something about me they didn't like—how little I communicated or was around when they thought I should be—and I knew that they didn't fully embrace the person I am. Their love for me would be contingent upon my compliance with what they desired from me, and conditional."

"You never met anyone worth the compromise?"

"I can't settle to not be satisfied, and spend my life conforming to someone else's needs. Either I'll encounter someone who doesn't need that from me, or come to a place where I no longer mind his need for my compromise, or be alone."

"You're willing to spend your life alone?"

"What's so wrong with that?"

"You don't want to grow old with someone?"

"I'll grow old with *every*one. Aging isn't improved by having a man in my bed. When I die, I can't take him with me. With all the marriages and divorces people have here on earth, if we were reunited with spouses in the afterlife, a lot of people would be polygamists when they got there."

"I've just never heard anyone—any woman—say the things you say."

"Most people chase what other people have. I chase what I desire to feel, and what I feel can't be determined by factors outside of me—including people."

"In other words, you're chasing yourself? Your own ability to make yourself happy?"

"What else is there to life than to enjoy the journey on your own terms, and to give love freely without expecting a return?"

~

It seems that she greatly desired joy and harmony, but what do you think Zoë liked least about her life during the time you were together?

I believe she was grateful for the job she had in the mall, but she never lit up when she talked about it. She was there part-time, about 3 to 4 days each week. The job was easy for her. The store was near to going out of business, so she only helped the few customers who trickled in on occasion. Children's toy stores aren't as popular as they once were.

That would be it--working in the toy store. At least, that was my observation. With Zoë, I measured how she felt about something by the expression on her face, or her body language. Unless she was making a point, she didn't have venting sessions about anything at all.

Do you believe Zoë was truthful when she explained how she perceived relationships?

Yes. Why would she lie? What would be the alternative?

If you were pursuing a relationship with her, it's possible for her to spare your feelings and tell you that she wasn't ready for a committed relationship.

That's true, but I wasn't pursuing her. I liked her, and enjoyed her company, but I didn't put any pressure on her, or what we had together.

It seems you knew all along that things weren't over between you and your wife.

I can't say I knew for sure, but I had doubts that things were completely over or beyond repair.

How did the end of your fling with Zoë come about--if you don't mind me asking?

I left Zoë's place on Christmas Eve to visit relatives in another state. Before I knew it, it was February, and I realized I hadn't seen or heard from Zoë for weeks. I assumed she needed to distance herself since we'd spent so much time together around the holidays. So, after I sent a few text messages that went unanswered, I backed off to give her space.

One evening, around that time, my wife called to invite me to her colleague's Wakanda party, which was hosted in response to the excitement surrounding the *Black Panther* film. She didn't want to go alone since couples were invited to wear costumes that exemplified African royalty. "I couldn't be Queen without my King," she said. There was sincerity in her voice, and I was curious to see where it would go.

I met her that evening. At some point, we escaped to a quiet room, and as she spoke, I listened. I felt the energy within each syllable she spoke, and I could recognize when she attempted to hold back or find better ways of saying something, but I let her. While I enjoyed the company of the woman I had taken as my bride, I couldn't help but think of the woman whose character I had learned to mimic—and was using it to woo my wife back to me.

After a week, I started to see my wife on a daily basis. We would meet for lunch, or she would stop by the office to drop something off to me. We weren't picking up where we left off; we were starting over. I didn't want the same wife who'd left me just as much as she no longer wanted the man she'd left, but we were both willing to make it work.

So, you abandoned Zoë and the baby to get back with your wife?

No, it wasn't like that. I didn't know Zoë was pregnant and, more than that, it was because of her that I won my wife back. She helped me to become selfless, to understand deeper than my own ego would allow. I finally understood what caused the rift in my marriage, and I fixed it. To some degree, that was because of Zoë.

I had developed feelings for Zoë. It was the way she would light up when she saw me, giggled at my jokes, listened attentively to my plans, and would nod even when she didn't understand them but could sense my immense passion. She was great, but she wasn't mine. She didn't belong to anyone. She was misplaced.

If I had known Zoë was pregnant, I don't think I would have gone back to my wife. A part of me thinks she knew that. And my decision would have been less about "bliss" and more about responsibility.

If I may ask, what was his name?

Who?

Your son? Zoë's son?

Wow—umm—sorry. Hearing that... He's never been referred to as my son. Excuse me a moment.

But umm—she named him Honest.

Thank you, again, for your time.
If you don't mind, please close my office door behind you. I need some time alone.

CHRISTINE RACHEAL

INTERVIEW FIVE

Date: Wednesday, January 15, 2020
Time: 8:05 PM
Location: Tallahassee, Florida

SOURCE: MARIE DOBSON

I followed her—on three different occasions. I'm not proud to say I did, but my husband had become a different man. And although I wasn't pleased by his methods, I was curious.

The girl worked at children's toy store in the mall, and I knew the exact location. Travis told me during the hour-long confession about his relationship with a "sweet" college student. I couldn't believe my husband had been with someone else while we were still legally committed to each other. When he confided in me, I was beyond furious but, over time, I was grateful he didn't hide it. My husband is far from perfect, but he's honest. To my knowledge, he didn't keep anything from me regarding her. He said he wanted to know that he won me back with the details of his full truth, and not lies.

The first time I went to see the girl my husband admitted to engaging with sexually, it was a Wednesday evening. I was already exhausted, and had gotten off from a long day at the bank; but the mall was only a 10-minute drive up the road. When I got there, I went to the west end of the mall and stood outside the store for a while, but didn't notice any employees. I had no time to waste, so I went inside and pretended to look at stuffed, blue unicorns that dangled on the back wall.

Suddenly, a man approached. "Good evening. Can I help you find something?" he asked.

"No. I'm just looking," I responded.

"The unicorns are on sale this week. You get half off the second one you purchase."

"Got it. Thanks."

"Let me know if you need anything," he said, and then walked away.

I continued to browse around the store, but the night was slow, and it appeared that only the associate who approached me was working. I moved closer to the register and heard something rattling behind it, but I didn't see anyone. I picked up a chocolate bar, or two, and pretended to read their nutritional value as I eyed the counter. Nothing. I put them down and walked closer. Quickly, a girl behind the counter stood to her feet, and we were immediately face to face.

"Hi," she said with a smile.

I returned the smile but kept moving.

She looked down at the counter and began to click the computer's mouse.

Her colleague approached. "Is it working now?"

"Looks like it's still stuck," she said. "We may have to get another one. I don't know if we can ring up any purchases."

"We're slow tonight. There's a device in the back. We can use it if anyone buys anything. Let me get it." He walked away.

The girl placed her hands at her hips. She gazed at the computer as if her stare could repair it, and then she noticed I was still there—within a few feet of the exit.

"I'm sorry. You need help with anything?" she asked.

"No. I think I'm fine. Thanks." I walked out.

I wasn't certain it was her. Travis had shared many details of their involvement, but he never described her. The girl in the store that evening was quite natural. Her hair was twisted on each side of her head and raised into a large, curly puff. Her eyebrows were neat and very full. Her skin was smooth and glowed a bit, but was without color—lipstick, blush, or eyeshadow. She was very pretty—fresh even. I would say we were opposites. I'm an attractive woman, but I was years older than her, loved a good weave, and was in my fourth year as a Mary Kay consultant, so I wore the brand daily. Again, I wasn't sure the girl I encountered in the store was Travis' old lover, so I went back.

The second time, I watched her from a small seating area comprised of contemporary chairs and a couch right in front of the store. I followed her movements as she handed a teddy bear to a young girl from a high shelf; and again, as she patiently escorted a mother with two overly-active children to the store's stock of coloring books, markers, and crayons.

It was June—a time when girls her age wear more revealing clothing to keep themselves cool. Although she was at work where shorts and tank tops would be out of dress code, her attire was fit for winter. She wore a loose-fitting, long-sleeved dress that hung over her knees. It was a shade of purple.

A customer walked into the store, and the girl turned abruptly to greet them. And that's when I saw it. As she shifted, her dress clung tightly to her body for a moment, and I noticed her belly. Such a small frame shouldn't have the extra weight in the middle, and I knew she was pregnant.

I kept my position in the mini-lounge area until closing time. Some of the lights inside the store flashed off, and the girl walked out before another employee lowered the gate at the entryway. I stood, and followed her from a good distance. The mall was nearly empty. Her pace was slow, which made it obvious she was in no hurry. After a few minutes, she walked into a restaurant at one of the mall's exits. There were about six tables of patrons who were being served, but the bar was empty. The girl took a seat at the bar.

I stood outside and contemplated what I would say if I went in—like I had a week earlier. A part of me wanted to write her off as something from Travis' past, but my curiosity about her wouldn't let me back out of the restaurant, or move me towards my car.

I walked in, skipped a single seat, and sat next to her at the bar. She massaged her neck and yawned—covering her mouth with the opposite hand. Her hair was pulled into a bun high on her head. If she was wearing any makeup that day, it was minimal. Even her lips had a soft, natural hue. She tugged at the short, curly hairs that swept across the back of her neck, and closed her eyes.

The bartender approached to take my order, and the girl looked in my direction. For a moment, I was shook. Without thinking, I blurted out, "Dirty martini," and the bartender went away.

The girl closed her eyes again, but opened them and fully came back into the room when the bartender placed her order in front of her. She stirred it a little with her straw, and then sipped the pinkish concoction from the glass.

"I see your situation," I said to her. She looked my way.

"Should you be drinking?"

"I don't drink. It's ginger ale. Splash of syrup."

I was stumped with what to say next. "I'm sure people would think…"

"What people think don't bother me." She looked strangely at me, "Do I know you?"

"No," I said initially, but immediately changed tunes. "I should be honest. I'm Marie Dobson. Travis' wife."

You could tell by her facial expression that she was stunned by my presence. Her eyebrows raised as she titled her head. I thought she would become angry and defensive, but she didn't. She looked deeply into my eyes and said, "You're as beautiful as he described you," and then she released a half-smile. She stirred her drink again.

I was caught off-guard and didn't know what to say to her. She took a few more gulps through the straw, stood up, and then removed a few dollars from her wristlet to pay for her drink.

"Don't leave," I said.

"It's not you. I'm tired."

There was no point in sugarcoating it. The elephant in the room had to die. "The baby?" I inquired.

She tugged at her dress to loosen the material around her belly.

"What about it?"

"So, you *are* pregnant. Is it—you know—Travis?"

"He doesn't know," she said. "And he doesn't have to. You're together again. I won't get in the way of that."

I wanted so badly to be angry, but she was indeed the "sweet" girl he described her to be. Through the devilish whispers from the other shoulder, my husband was in the dark about her condition, and I couldn't be nice. Bitterness seeped deep into heart as I digested the situation; the girl responsible for my "better" husband, was also carrying his child.

She placed the money on the counter. "Tell Travis I said, 'Hi'."

I responded, "I don't pass love notes to my husband, but you take care."

She breathed deeply, lowered her eyes, and walked away.

I never told my husband about what I had discovered.

~

How would you describe your relationship with your husband?

We've gone through quite a bit within the five years we've been married, but we're solid. When I left him two years ago, it wasn't because he was a bad guy. He was always loyal and caring. I never feared he would sleep around or deceive me in any way, but he wasn't giving me what I thought I needed from him. When we came back together, he met me halfway. I had to discover a healthy need for him; and at the same time, he learned to give me the attention I needed to feel like we were on the same team. Without it, there was no point being married to each other.

Did you ever suspect he was with someone else after you left?

Work was my husband's lover. I thought he would be as consumed by it after I left as he was when we were together. If he didn't have the time to spend with *me*, where would he find a moment to entertain or pursue someone else? We spoke casually after I left, but he didn't mention her. It wasn't until we officially decided to get back together that he told me.

You said your husband was honest about his relationship with Zoë. Did he ever share how he felt about her?

Not exactly. He was invested enough to let her in, and she was able to influence him in ways that I possibly could have had he opened up to me. Or…perhaps he *didn't* open up more for her. Maybe she just had a way of reaching people. I don't know. I would say he liked her, but not "love". If he loved the girl, he wouldn't have come back to me.

What made you withhold the news of Zoë's pregnancy from him?

What could it help? Nothing. If she didn't want to ruin *my* marriage with him knowing, why the hell would I? I wanted to put it all behind us, and I respected her desire to do the same.

You truly believe it was something she wanted? To keep him in the dark about his baby?

Travis told me that while they were dealing with each other, she wasn't the most accessible person. He said it was *her* that stopped communicating with *him*. If she wanted to involve Travis, the girl could have said something. As much as I would've hated it, I know him, and Travis wouldn't have left her out there alone. Yes, I knew about it, but it was not my responsibility.

How could you not feel a duty, a responsibility, to protect your husband by letting him know another woman was carrying his baby?

How could that protect him? Travis is a grown ass man. What about his duty to protect me, or our marriage?

In every way, I understand what you've said; but consider what would have happened if she had popped up at any point and shared the news with him.

I chose to take my chances and keep him in the dark. What he didn't know wouldn't hurt him.

But it did.

Yeah. But it hurt me first. After they died, his pain could not be avoided. If you're fishing for my regrets, you can go ahead and fall back. I don't have any. In this situation, I was nothing more than an innocent bystander. It wasn't my fault. None of it. I didn't tell him to go out there and get the girl pregnant. It was because I loved him that I stayed after I found out. I could have left him then, but I didn't want to give some random girl the power to decide the fate of my marriage. If I left, it would be because I wanted to.

You didn't know Zoë personally, but based on your encounter and what you've heard, were her circumstances enough to drive her over the edge?

You're right. I didn't know the girl personally, so I can't say what would drive her over the edge. I can say this: I've known girls to deal with much less and really have a hard time adjusting. Having a baby is one thing. Having a baby with a man who's not around is another. Having a baby with a man who's not around, *and* who's married to someone else, is pretty fucked up. Add to that: working to pay bills and keeping up in school. I'm sure the combination can drive anyone to do things they never imagined they would.

INTERVIEW SIX

Date: Thursday, January 16, 2020
Time: 11:32 AM
Location: Tallahassee, Florida

SOURCE: MANDY SMITH

How did you come to know Zoë?

First, through her foster mother, Gayle, who is a really good friend of mine. We're both from south Florida and graduates of a university down there. Ultimately, I landed a role here, but we've remained good friends. Second, I was Zoë's academic advisor since she started at the university.

How often did you see her?

Not too often. Typically, when she reached a new classification—-moving from freshman to sophomore, and so forth. Zoë was intelligent, witty; she was the kind of girl who could figure things out on her own. She chose a major she could enjoy, and would lead her to law school, and stuck with it. She wasn't like students who switch majors and concentrations on a whim.

What would you say motivated Zoë?

Zoë wasn't motivated; she was inspired. The thing that drove her to make decisions about courses and activities didn't come from other people or outside forces. It came from within her. The colors, or bonds, or outward friendliness of campus organizations, wasn't enough to convince Zoë to do anything. Her decisions were based on whether they felt good enough to do them.

I gave her a questionnaire during freshman year, and it asked who she admired most, or who she aspired to be like—or something like that. In response, she wrote that she most wanted to be herself.

What was Zoë like academically?

She came here from high school bordering on a 4.0. In college courses, she was above average, but not excellent. She consistently earned a 'B' in most of her courses, and had an 'A' sprinkled in here and there. It was very possible for Zoë to have a 4.0 at this level. It's not that she didn't apply herself enough to attain it; she merely refused to push beyond certain limits.

I helped select courses that appealed to her, and I believe she showed up and did her absolute best. However, showing up was all she was prepared to do. Zoë told me that she always actively engaged in discussions and groups, submitted each assignment by deadlines, completed home-based activities, and the result would still yield a 'B'. I suggested study groups and tutoring if she wanted to reach for the 4.0. With her grades, it wasn't necessary, but I wanted to encourage her to take advantage of those resources. She said something along the lines of, "I'm completely focused during lectures, I cover the reading materials my professors assign, and I complete 100% of the coursework. Whatever I earn is what I deserve."

She wasn't interested in impressing anyone with excellent grades—not even herself. If she made an 'A' in a course, she attributed it to the idea that she was just a natural or had found more interest in it, and not because she had worked harder.

Was she able to maintain her academic performance the entire time she was enrolled here?

Surprisingly, yes. She wavered towards the end, but she committed to getting back on track.

~

Zoë reached senior status by the end of summer 2018, and was on track to graduate within two semesters. It was November, and we were at least a month away from concluding the fall session when Zoë unexpectedly stopped by for a visit.

During Zoë's previous appointment at the end of summer, we outlined the final semesters leading to graduation. She was about seven months along in her pregnancy, and as optimistic and vibrant as ever. At her final visit, she wasn't the same Zoë I had observed and spoken with before. I can't call it depression, because her emotions weren't sad or hopeless in nature; but for the first time, she didn't have all the answers. And that was unlike her.

Although she had recently delivered a baby, when she came into my office, Zoë was thin. I've heard that women her age, whose bodies have only experienced a single child birth, bounce back quickly; but Zoë was thinner than before she ever carried a baby.

"Hey, Zoë," I said when she entered my office. "How can I help you today? And how's the baby?"

She smiled. "He's good, Ms. Smith. Thanks for asking." She sat in the chair across from my desk. "I came for some advice."

"Okay."

She settled into the chair. "I've been away for a few weeks because of the baby. Before I left, I didn't drop any of my classes, so I'm still enrolled."

"But you've missed a significant amount of coursework."

"Yes."

"You can easily withdraw from your courses and speak with the dean about receiving incompletes. I'm sure your situation would qualify you."

"I know. I thought of that. The thing is—I don't want to push this semester's course load back—at least not all of them."

"Give me a second to pull up your transcript."

I turned to my computer to retrieve the information I needed while Zoë sat quietly.

"You're enrolled in 15 hours—good God, child. That's a lot at this level."

She stared, awaiting my recommendation.

"You're right," I said. "I don't know how you would be able to complete these courses successfully this semester. So, let's do a bit of both. I would say, first, talk with your professors. Some may be open to helping you make up what you've missed; but please understand, they are not required to do so. Don't take it personal if they refuse."

Zoë nodded her head.

"Once you identify which professors are not willing to assist, I would speak with the dean about receiving an incomplete in their courses." She was far from excited after my statement. "It's just one additional semester, Zoë. What's the rush?"

"No rush, but I committed to finishing on time."

"Things change, Zoë. And some things are beyond our control."

"Yeah. Things change, but I can't believe it's beyond my control."

I looked at a girl who was hopeful, and determined to have her way.

"Are you still working part-time?"

"No," Zoë said.

"What happened there?"

"Initially, I took some time off after having Honest. I was only part-time, so there wasn't any maternity leave. The manager was gracious enough to say he would bring me back afterwards anyway; but by the time I was ready, he had already filled the position to get ready for holiday shoppers."

"How are you managing your expenses then?"

"I'm working it out. I still have a little something from the second scholarship I received."

"Formula? Diapers? Have you talked to Gayle about this?"

I knew the answer before I asked. Gayle, my close friend, had been Zoë's foster mother in the years leading up to Zoë's college enrollment, and she was still very invested in her success. Gayle had the resources to help Zoë, and she would have. That was a fact.

"No," she responded.

"Why not? You need the help."

"She's already done a lot for me. She doesn't deserve the burden."

"That's silly. You're not a burden. You know she wouldn't mind. She loves you, Zoë."

"I know, but I mind." She stood from her chair. "It will all come together. It will. I'll keep you posted on what my professors say about finishing the semester."

"Okay then."

She walked towards me as I sat behind my desk. "Give me a hug," she said sweetly and extended her arms.

Her request was so unexpected. We never hugged at previous visits, but I stood, and we embraced.

"Thank you," she said, and then she left.

~

Did you tell your friend, Zoë's foster mother, about her situation?

No. For a while after she died, I regret that I didn't. At the time, I understood her reason to not involve Gayle. Zoë was so filled with gratitude for how well Gayle cared for her that she settled on some idea that she had already done enough--and maybe the idea that she no longer needed Gayle. Secondly, Zoë was one of the rare success stories; she made it all the way to college in spite of some horrific childhood adversities. I think exposing her dilemma would cast a shadow on that success. She may have been prideful, but I never thought it would lead to this. Otherwise, I would have called Gayle the very day Zoë came into my office.

Did you see Zoë again after that meeting?

No, I didn't. She sent me an email that said only one of her literature professors would permit her to complete the semester. She was okay with it because she could focus solely on that course and get it done. The dean had also approved her request for "incompletes".

Did she seem discouraged in her communication with you?

No, it was quite the opposite. I think having a solution made her feel better. She discovered what she could do about it, moved forward, and accepted it. The instructor who permitted Zoë to complete the semester was Dr. Gregory. He may be able to give some insight as well. He has office hours right now if you want to catch him.

Interview Seven

Date: Thursday, January 16, 2020
Time: 1:43 PM
Location: Tallahassee, Florida

SOURCE: DR. ROBERT GREGORY

There were about 70 students enrolled in my literature course in the fall of 2018. It was early in the semester, and I hadn't interacted with many of them on an individual basis; and was seldom able to match a face with a name. However, I could match a name with a student's work, and Zoë's work was so impressive that it was hard to forget. On a rainy Tuesday afternoon, I was finally able to match the work of an amazing student with her face.

It was after 5 o'clock when I left campus for the day. I was in the car, and perhaps two miles from campus, when I passed a young lady on the side of the road. Her car's hood was raised, and she was walking back to the driver's seat to get in. Her face was familiar, and I quickly recognized her as a current student of mine, but it was the first time I noticed her condition. With her fully round, protruding belly, she was obviously in the latter phase of pregnancy. I had never been close enough to notice.

I circled around the block and carefully pulled up behind her. I grabbed my umbrella and immediately got out to offer my assistance. She sat in her car and looked straight ahead. It wasn't dark enough for headlights, so mine weren't on, and she hadn't noticed my arrival. I knocked on her window slightly, and it startled her.

"Dr. Gregory?" she said, puzzled.

"Do you need some help?"

She gazed upon the front of her car, and then slowly shook her head. "No. I'll be fine."

"Is it overheating?" I asked.

She finally rolled down her window.

"No. It's been in and out of the shop. Different issues. She's pretty old. I'm good though. Thank you so much."

"I'm sorry. Tell me your name."

"I'm Zoë."

"Zoë Sapp?"

"Yes, sir." She gripped her steering wheel with both hands as she looked up at me.

"Ah, okay. Try starting your car." She turned the key in the ignition. Silence.

"I've tried a few times," she said, and then the rain became heavier.

"It may not start tonight—or at all. Where do you live?"

"About 3 miles from here."

"Can I offer you a ride home?"

"No, thanks. I'll be fine."

"Can you call someone to come and get you?"

"No. There should be a bus. If I see one coming this way, I'll get on it."

"It means you'll have to stand out here in the rain. It's no bother—really."

She observed her surroundings as though I wasn't standing there waiting for her response.

"Zoë, if you're concerned, I can call my wife at home. She can talk to you until I get you there safely," I assured her. "Or you can call someone yourself. I would like to know you made it indoors. It'll be dark soon. You're pregnant and—."

"I'll just walk," she said, and grabbed a shoulder bag from the passenger's seat. She removed the keys from the ignition and tossed them into the bag. Her hand reached for the door handle, so I moved out of the way.

She opened the door, stepped out, and went to close the car's hood. "Thank you anyway," she said with a faint smile.

"You don't have an umbrella?" I called out to her.

"No. I left it at home," she said as she squinted to shield her eyes from the rain.

"Here. Take mine." I extended it towards her.

"I can't do that."

"It won't hurt. I'm going straight from the car into the garage. I don't need it. Here."

She finally grabbed it. "Thank you. I'll get it back to you as soon as I can."

"No worries. Get home safely."

"I will." She turned to walk away, and never once looked back.

I thought her behavior was bizarre. I don't go around looking to pick up young women stranded on the side of the road, but I assumed those conditions would make anyone open to receive some assistance. She wasn't.

Zoë seemed heavily guarded, but pleasant. Perhaps her refusal to accept my help was due to some inability to perceive me as anything more than her superior, a professor who should avoid mingling with female students beyond campus. I can't say for sure what she thought of me, but I genuinely tried to help her.

The following afternoon, I was reviewing recently submitted essays when there was a knock on my opened, office door. It was Zoë.

"Dr. Gregory," she said as she entered. "I came to return this to you." She handed the umbrella over to me.

I stood from my desk. "Thank you. I told you it wasn't a big deal."

"I know. I would rather not hold on to something that doesn't belong to me for too long."

"It's just an umbrella."

"*Your* umbrella."

"Okay. I won't argue with that. How's the car?" I asked.

"Still there. I should be able to find someone to tow it after my next class."

"How did you get to campus today?"

"Walked. I don't mind. I get in some exercise and rest better in the evenings."

"I can understand that. My wife worked out almost every day until her eighth month with both of her pregnancies. Nothing strenuous—just walking, stretching, lifting light weights. When the babies became too heavy and made it uncomfortable to work out, she slowed down."

I tried to make small talk, but I could tell by how Zoë's body was positioned, angled slightly towards the door, that she didn't plan to stay long.

"I guess I'm not there yet." She rubbed her belly, and then

looked up suddenly as if she'd had an epiphany. "Can I ask you a question?"

"Sure," I said.

"I was talking to a guy who took your course last semester, and he randomly said that you're racist, but against white people—and you're white."

I laughed a little on the inside because I knew the source of the anonymous student's comment.

"I'll explain it this way. For 20 years, I taught at Albany State. I retired, and came here. From our classroom, I can see FAMU sitting up on the hill. And sometimes, I wish I was there instead."

"I get it," she said.

"Do you need help finding a company?"

"A company? For what?"

"To tow your car."

"Right. No, thanks. I got it." She started for the door.

"Are you sure? Towing is an expense—especially when you add it to the cost of repairs. It's not easy on a student's budget."

"Yeah, but some guys around here will tow it for free if I hire them to make the repairs."

"Seems like you got it all figured out."

"For now," she said, and left my office.

Zoë was in class another four weeks after that day. She was always there when I arrived—somewhere around the third or fourth row—and I understood how I had missed the fact that she was pregnant. She was in the classroom and already seated behind her desk when I arrived; and she blended with others to leave when they were dismissed.

Despite her condition, Zoë never missed a day, or fell asleep, or asked to leave early. She always had a snack though. She would have pretzels one day, kale chips or dried bananas the next, but I didn't mind. It was amazing to see a student that late in her pregnancy continue to attend class—trekking up and down hills from one building to another. She was the first for me. Although I didn't know her personally, I silently applauded her effort. I was happy she didn't quit. It took a lot of courage to walk this campus in her condition and not miss a beat, hang her head, disappear altogether, or simply have the baby disappear.

The day came when Zoë wasn't in the room at the start of class. It was the first week of October, and the air outside had become crisp and comforting. The seasons were changing, and so was Zoë. After her second absence, I assumed she had gone into labor, and would be at home with her newborn for some time. If she was able, I knew she would have been there.

~

Did you hear from Zoë while she was away with the baby?

Yes. About a week after her first string of absences, she sent an email that confirmed she had delivered the baby, and stated she was not prepared to drop her classes. She said she would follow up with each of her professors after a few weeks to see what her options were.

Did you extend an opportunity for Zoë to continue in your course?

She was incredibly behind, but why wouldn't I let her try? Make-up work piled on top of current work is a headache for any educator, so I seldom give students the opportunity. Zoë was different. She was hardworking and focused, and I wanted her to make it work. Besides, other professors had turned her down. She told me so in a response email after I approved the extension. It was unfortunate, but it meant she would have time to focus solely on the work she had to complete for my course. Her chances of success were improved.

~

Zoë was a good student—focused, diligent, respectable. She stretched her thinking and consistently sought understanding—not of what I taught in class, but *why* I taught it. She declared that anything presented to a body of people created an argument intended to unearth something within them, or cause them to act in a certain manner—across every medium, even fiction. Every short story or novel we covered in class was met with, "How do you want this work to impact us? How could it alter the lives of your students?" In response, I referred to possible purposes the author could have had based on context, or what was taking place in history at the time it was written.

Zoë responded, "That's why they wrote it, but why do you want us to read it?"

"It deepens your understanding of conflicts within that era, and reveals how people either coped, or thrived."

"So, there's nothing in this book that can alter my perspective on life in 2018?"

"Yes, there are several themes in the book that are consistently demonstrated in each of our lives."

"And the novel will help us progress in a positive direction?"

"It depends on how you receive its content."

"Aha!" She smiled big. "You can't tell me how I'll respond to a work. Right?" she smirked. "Mark David Chapman believed a fictional character—one who despised the 'phony' wealthy—would have desired to kill John Lennon, and committed his murder. The power of fiction is very evident, Dr. Gregory."

I responded, "Chapman's attorneys also used an insanity defense during his trial—stating that God told him to do it."

"Insanity is subjective. To this day, many biblical characters are applauded by Christians—including those ordered by God to destroy lives. I'm not justifying murder, but saying you hear God doesn't make you insane. Great tactic by his attorneys though."

After a few minutes, and some engagement from other students, our discussion ended.

Don't get me wrong. As far as I could tell, Zoë's intent wasn't to challenge my authority or to bump heads with me, or with other students for that matter. She knew the American literature curriculum was provided by the university; but she questioned why I would choose one book over another, or she would contribute how an author's skewed perception, or misconceptions casted shadows over the arguments within their works.

Ultimately, Zoë's desire to know why we make the choices we do, stretched me too. In addition to those instances, Zoë liked to play what I call "angel's advocate", which intensified our classroom discussions. No matter how gruesome the acts being discussed were, or how villainous the characters, she always found good or innocence within them. It would set off a few students on occasion; their expectation was for everyone to understand and agree that an incident or character was unworthy or despicable. Zoë understood, but would seldom agree. One day, during a heated debate, she asked,

"Is it not possible for imperfect people to be victims too?" Her question caused many wheels in the room to spin. She was a deep thinker, and very observant. And her writing—Zoë had a way of writing objectively in truth, but was so passionate about what she spoke that it seemed personal. She had a gift.

On Wednesday evenings, I opened one of the lecture halls for a bible club I sponsored to meet. The time and location worked for Zoë; she said it was the only evening she could get a sitter for her newborn each week. We agreed that she would pick up with my lectures on Tuesday and Thursday afternoons, and make up previous assignments and exams on Wednesday evenings.

At the top of December, we had our third make-up session. Zoë worked quietly to complete a character analysis of Charlotte Brontë's *Jane Eyre* when bible club students entered the room.

They assembled near the front—at least twenty-five of them that evening—and began their meeting. I was sure Zoë could hear their discussion, but whenever I glanced in her direction, she was staring down at her paper.

About a half hour into their meeting, the conversation shifted from scriptural references and maintaining a clean lifestyle on campus, to an all-out rant about the behaviors of other students.

"I mean the guy wasn't ashamed either," a female student spoke from her seat. "He sat in my ASL class and announced to everyone in our section that he is an atheist."

"More and more students are doing that—claiming atheist or agnostic beliefs. They don't even know what it all means," another guy responded.

"All I know is that I switched seats the following class. Devil worshipping is definitely against what we believe."

"Yes. The Bible tells us to judge a spirit, and to not be unequally yoked—that includes every relationship, even the ones we have in school. We were set apart for His purpose. So, you're right to separate yourself from nonbelievers. That's why we have these meetings—for us to connect and support each other. We've been called by God to be the light on this campus."

Someone else spoke, "It's hard to do with all the gay and lesbian organizations, and other programs, the school permits. There are even organizations of straight people created just to say they support gay people. It's insane. We look like the bad guys when the administration condones it."

"And they take it personal too. I find myself saying, 'Look, I don't hate you. I hate the sin.' That's truly how I see it. I feel the same way about students who smoke weed or drink alcohol. It's not the person, but the behavior I can't stand."

"The tough ones are those who really think they're born that way. I went back and forth with a guy who said he knew he was gay when he was four years old. He wondered why God would hate him for feeling something so strongly at an age when he couldn't have known it was wrong."

"And how did that conversation end?" another student asked.

"It didn't. I just told him that God loves him. I couldn't think of anything else."

"And that would be right," came boldly from a distant voice.

The club members turned to see who had spoken, and Zoë, still looking at her paper, said, "That is probably the best thing spoken by any of you all night."

She had inserted herself, but she didn't disrupt the meeting, which, by campus policy, was open to all. So, I didn't stop her from speaking. I was curious to see where she would go.

The group's leader addressed her, "What are you saying? That everything we've mentioned—being gay, atheist, or an alcoholic—is okay?"

Some students in the group shook their heads, and others shifted in their seats to hear what the girl in the back of the room had to say.

She looked at them. "I'm saying that even acknowledging those traits in other people puts you in direct violation of your own biblical commandment—judgement."

"It's not judgement; it's observation. And we were called to be light so that the darkness would flee."

"Or perhaps light should ignite more light. Why do you carry the weight of ridding the world of what you deem unacceptable and unlovable? The truth is that no matter how far you move your seat from the atheist, you're still bound to him by the absolute fact that your Creator is one in the same. If you claim there is only one God, did your God not create him too?"

"Yes, but not to turn on Him and serve the devil."

Zoë continued, "Not all atheists practice what you call "devil-worship". Atheist don't believe in the supernatural. They're limited to what they can see and experience in their natural form."

"But the Word says we can't serve two masters, and that we must be either hot or cold for Christ."

"And you believe moving your seat proves that to someone who doesn't even care? Does that help him to believe in the supernatural?"

"We pray for all the lost souls out there. We don't have to be friends to do that. Jesus will save them."

"No, that's *your* job, not God's. Pointing out what you've categorized as character flaws, may give you a sense of unity amongst other believers, but that wasn't what Jesus commanded you to do. If I remember correctly, after being baptized, his first call was for people to repent," Zoë said.

"Exactly! We should all want to enter his kingdom in heaven."

"Another misconception. The kingdom isn't a place you ascend to after you die. The kingdom of God is how you think, and treat others, while you live on earth. The kingdom of God is right where you stand. When he said, 'Repent, for the kingdom of God is at hand', he meant that men and women need to change how they think so that they can align with what will be done through them on earth. It had less to do with their sins than you think. Two other commands Jesus gave was to follow him, and to love one another. Based on your discussion, you're not in alignment with either of them. That's not judgement either; just my observation."

"We all do our best to keep the commandments and to love one another."

"You only love who you think is loveable. If you were a true follower of Christ, your mission would be to find a loveable element in *all* people, and to withhold judgment of the things that are not—especially when it's based on your culturally-engrained standards, or comes from your very subjective lens."

"I don't believe that. It is our duty to win souls for His glory."

"Or yours. And soul-winning? Is it a roster of people who approached a church altar, or who said a prayer of repentance? You believe these people *never* return to unfruitful, unrighteous behaviors? They never lie, or cheat, or steal? They never fornicate, commit adultery, or fantasize about men or women outside of their marriages? Once you've won their souls, they forever avoid destructive behaviors, right?" Zoë asked.

"Not exactly. They have a choice."

"Okay. If soul-winning, which you've said is your purpose as a believer, isn't the end all be all to their soul's journey, then why do you place so much emphasis on doing something that will very easily be undone?" She paused. "To truly save someone, you must show them how to think differently, to see themselves as spirit-beings inhabiting fleshly bodies, and to use the body and their conscious mind as tools to navigate the journey. But you can't do that by judging, pointing fingers, making them feel ostracized. You do it by loving them where they are, and without some concealed intent to move them to where you *think* they should be. It's not your place, nor your purpose. That's why Jesus said to love each other was the greatest of his commands. It's not so easy to do."

Zoë smirked, and then shrugged at the onlookers. She grabbed her pen from the desk, and returned to her assignment. The meeting continued, but more quietly.

~

Was Zoë always so outspoken in a classroom setting?

Yes, she was, but not aggressively. Something had to provoke Zoë to speak. She would listen as conversations went in complete circles and back again before she would inject her own opinion. She respectfully waited for everyone to have a turn—-and sometimes a few turns—-before she shared her thoughts.

Were other students typically in agreement with her?

Agreement, no. Respected her insight, yes. It was hard for many of them to fully grasp what Zoë contributed to class discussions. That was made obvious when a student would respond to her statements with something that was completely unaligned with what she'd spoken. She didn't repeat herself, or offer additional clarity. It takes a lot to accept that others simply don't get it, and resist the urge to force them to.

What would you say was Zoë's weakness?

Personally: Based on my experience with her, I would say it was her stubbornness—-her unwillingness to receive my help. I didn't know her enough to understand why she was that way, but there must have been a reason. I guess she preferred to hold out until she really needed a hand; and I was ready and willing to give her the one she needed to complete my course.

In the classroom setting: I would say her weakness was her presence.

You mean, Zoë shouldn't have been in the class?

Not in that way. Zoë had a strong, unapologetic presence. She could be intimidating. I don't fault her for it. It's something she couldn't turn off, and was her nature. Unfortunately, her reality was hard for other students to grasp. I could understand how she would be an outsider and, quite frankly, she was.

When was the last time you saw Zoë?

I had office hours on Wednesdays, Thursdays, and Fridays. The Friday before winter break, she ran into my office to drop off her final make-up assignment. She had successfully completed the work in my course in spite of welcoming a baby in the middle of it.

What was she like when you saw her?

She was usually really calm, but when I saw her that day, she seemed hurried. It was at the top of my office hours, so I knew the rush wasn't for me. It was obvious she wanted to get somewhere because she walked out as quickly as she walked in.

Did you believe Zoë would kill herself?

When I heard the news, it tore me up. It was hard to believe a student of her caliber would do something like that. Not even a month before she died, she had worked diligently to complete assignments for a course she could have easily put on hold until the following semester, or dropped altogether. Zoë had plans of finishing college. It showed in those actions alone. I can't understand what could happen within a month's time that would drastically push her into the deep end.

INTERVIEW EIGHT

Date: Thursday, January 16, 2020
Time: 3:21 PM
Location: Tallahassee, Florida

SOURCE: "NEIGHBOR"

What can you tell me about Zoë?

Listen, I don't want to go on record—-at least not my name. It's been hard enough with all the attention this area received after they found the bodies. Occasionally, random kids will come snooping around here. I just want some peace. Okay?

I've lived here for over 8 years. My children are grown, so I live alone. I've had all sorts of neighbors over the years—-some good, some bad—-but I didn't mind Zoë being there at all. I could hear her the day she moved in. I heard when she would head out some mornings, and return in the evening, but that was all. Actually, I heard her music on occasion—-the sound of trumpets and bass—- but she couldn't help it. These walls are very thin.

Eventually, I bumped into her as we were both leaving home one day and introduced myself. She seemed like a nice girl, and kept to herself, mostly.

Did you notice any friends or boyfriends hanging around?

I ran into a young lady one day as I came up the walkway. She had on a dress, and was rolled tight. I may have only seen the girl a time or two after that, but I heard her voice echo from next door more times than I could count. She never gave me any trouble, but she made her presence known with her loud-talking.

Boyfriends? I can't say I did.

Did you ever see Zoë's baby?

Honest? Yeah, of course. He was one of the most adorable babies I've ever known—-and a real sweetie pie, but the boy had a set of lungs on him.

~

A few days had passed since the baby's arrival from the hospital with Zoë. I knew by the sounds that came from next door. It was early October. I was up one evening, catching up on one of my favorite Netflix series, when I heard the baby crying. The crying began somewhere around 8 o'clock, and by 10 I could still hear him. He would stop a few minutes, and then the crying would start again. By midnight, I was certain something was wrong. Perhaps she had left him alone over there, or had fallen into a deep sleep and left him to fend for himself.

I put on my housecoat and some slippers, and went to see what was happening. As I approached her front door, I could see light shining through a gap in the curtains. I stepped closer to the window and looked inside. She was there, but without a shirt or bra. Both of her breasts were exposed, but she had placed a towel across one of her shoulders, and she carried her baby in her arms. She calmly paced the floor, trying to get him to quiet down and to take her breast into his mouth, but he resisted. I thought to go back into my house and let the girl figure it out, but with six children of my own, I wanted to offer my help.

I knocked on the door. It took her a while to appear, but I was patient, knowing she would have to cover up before answering. When she got there, she wore a t-shirt, and the baby was no longer in her arms.

"I'm sorry. Did he wake you?" Zoë asked.

"No, I've been up a while. But he's been crying for some time now."

"He's alright, I think. No fever. He's just fussy."

"Not crying like that. What's he doing?" I asked. "Can I see him?"

She opened the door. Honest was screaming from the sofa.

"I've been trying to get him to eat, but I don't think he's getting anything."

I picked up the baby, sat down on the sofa, and examined him. He was red from all the fussing, but was otherwise physically okay. He gestured by moving his tiny fist across his mouth, and stopped to suck on it. I quickly understood his dilemma.

"When was the last time he had a bottle?"

"I haven't started pumping for him to use bottles."

"And he's sucking good from your breasts?"

"I don't know. Maybe not," she shrugged. "He'll get it in there, suck for a little while, and then he'll start crying again."

"Then he's not getting what he wants."

Zoë sat close to me and the baby. She gently rubbed his head with a *shhh*.

"Do you have any formula?"

"No. We used a little at the hospital, but I want to breastfeed."

"If you want to see if I can help, we can try; but some of these things we don't have control over."

Initially, she appeared discouraged, but after the moment had passed, she partly lifted her shirt and removed one of her breasts.

"Can you show me?" she asked.

"Here. Take him. Hold him good with this arm, but you'll

need to hold your breast as well to guide him." She struggled a little, so I picked up a pillow from the floor and placed it on her lap, which raised him closer to her breast.

"Squeeze out a little milk, first. He can smell it and taste it to know where he needs to be."

The poor thing squeezed, and very little came out.

"Do it again," I told her.

She squeezed again. That time, nothing. I wanted to see if Honest could pull something from her breasts anyway, and I didn't want to ruin her hopes so soon.

"Lift him a little closer to you. Now, he's going to find the milk, and when he opens wide, push as much of your nipple into his mouth as you can. Otherwise, it will hurt like hell."

He stopped fussing enough to open his mouth and latch perfectly to her breast. I was hopeful the issue had been resolved. He stayed there for about two minutes, and then he released the nipple and started to cry again. I suggested there wasn't enough milk in that breast, and told her to try the other. We went through each step again. He latched, sucked for a minute, let go and wailed.

"You may not have much in there." I said, and grabbed the baby from her lap to soothe him; but he was hungry and couldn't be comforted. "You'll have to get this baby some formula."

She attempted to hold back her tears, but they had already surfaced.

"I know how you feel, but what's important is that he eats."

She adjusted her bra to support her breasts and pulled down her shirt. "I have to go to the store," she said, and reached for the baby.

I would have offered to go myself, but my vision isn't good in the dark and I refuse to drive at night.

"You can't take him out—especially like this. Go, and hurry back so he can eat."

She hesitated. I didn't take offense because I knew I was a stranger to her.

"I've had six of these, and I live right next door. He's fine," I told her.

She went to her room for a pair of shoes and her keys, and she made a dash for the door.

All I could do was hold him while he cried. Anything else would have upset him more and, ultimately, the both of us. I wished I could as least stare at a television program, but noticed she didn't have a television—just a record player. So, I stared at him. He was a beautiful boy with a head full of dark hair that was straight in most places and stuck out at his neck. He had a little birthmark on one of his ankles that resembled the state of Texas.

Zoë returned after twenty minutes and quickly prepped his bottle in the kitchen. I stood by and watched to ensure everything was the right temperature and the materials were clean. She wanted his crying to stop, and for him to be satisfied, but she spared no chance of germs or bacteria getting to her baby. She was thorough. I could tell she loved him.

She sat down, and I handed Honest over to his mother. Zoë shook the bottle, and then slid it into his mouth. He was immediately comforted. You could see her light up. The breastfeeding blues was lifted. It wasn't just relief she experienced in that moment, but joy. She was happy to see him satisfied.

"I'll head back over," I said. "Looks like you got it."

"Thank you so much. You didn't have to do this."

"Well, it was this, or I would never hear how Lip is doing in AA on *Shameless*," I joked, but she didn't laugh. She had no clue what I was referring to. "If you need anything, I'm right next door. Don't try to figure it out on your own. It's a lot."

"Yes ma'am," she said.

"Come and lock the door before he falls asleep. You should be able to lay him down after burping him good. Forget to burp him, and you'll be right back where you started. Only, you'll have to help him get rid of gas instead."

She chuckled, and stood to show me out.

"Goodnight," she said.

~

Did Zoë ever ask for help after that night?

I would say I offered, and she accepted. I went over to visit her and the baby one day, and she told me she wanted to complete her fall classes, but didn't know how she could with the baby. She needed help, so I shared my schedule with her. I was open every day except Tuesdays and Thursdays when I would stay over at my mother's, who is up in age. Her caregiver wasn't available on those two days, so I would fill in since I don't work. I receive just enough from my pension to afford this place for myself, some groceries, and gas for my car when I need to go to Mom's.

But I didn't have babies anymore. I was a single parent most of their lives, but raised them to pursue the life they wanted. Each of them followed my instruction. My oldest was almost forty, and my baby was twenty-six. I didn't have any grandchildren, and I wanted them. Having Honest on days Zoë went to school was good for me, and I enjoyed him greatly. She was grateful for me, but I was also being blessed.

From your perspective, what kind of mother was Zoë?

A caring one. It may have been too early to truly tell, but I don't believe there was anything she wouldn't have done for him. I think a lot of young ladies are burdened by motherhood. Even though she was in the final stages of getting a college degree, I never heard her say a negative word against him or her situation.

One day, she wanted to feed him before dropping him off at my house. I guess she rushed the process, and he hadn't been properly burped. Let's just say she got him to the front door and he left a nice package dripping down her neck, onto her blouse, and down her back. I waited for her to have a fit. She kissed him instead, and held him up in the air. "Is that the kind of love you want to give today?" she said. "I'm sure I won't forget it."

I asked if she was going back over to change. She handed him to me, and used a burp cloth from his bag to wipe her neck. "It'll dry," is all she said before she left.

~

Honest was barely eight weeks old, and Zoë was able to attend an hour-long class on three days each week, and a session on Wednesday evenings. I didn't mind the baby's company. He slept mostly, and if he awoke, he only wanted a bottle or to be cuddled before lying down again. I didn't want to spoil the boy, especially with a young mother who would need the space to move about. So, whatever waking moment he would allow, I sat him in his carrier on my living room floor, and he would watch a television program with me. That is how Honest and I spent our 2-hour visits.

One day, little man completely exploded in his diaper, and I gathered the materials to change him—wipes, protective cream, a fresh diaper—and I laid him on a blanket across the couch.

"Hmmm. Someone's stinky," I said, waving my hand friskily in front of my face. He stared at me with the largest, adorable eyes as I loosened his diaper.

"My goodness, boy." I lifted his legs to get a clean wipe and folded it into his dirty diaper.

There was a knock on the door just a few feet away.

"Now, don't you go nowhere," I told him.

I opened the door for Zoë. I never expected any other visitors. My children always called before coming over.

"How is he?" she asked. She got a whiff of his stench. "Ew! Is that him?"

"You should be asking how *I'm* doing. This boy's funky butt is about to drive me out of town." I opened the clean diaper and slid it underneath him.

Zoë walked into my kitchen and grabbed a plastic grocery bag. "I won't torture you with this." She put the poopy diaper into the bag and tied it tightly. "I'll drop it in the garbage when I leave."

I continued to put diaper cream on Honest's bottom. "Feel good, huh."

Zoë sat on the edge of the sofa and glanced up at the television. "What are you watching?" she asked.

I looked at the screen. "Your president is threatening to shut down the government if he can't have his way with that wall. Can't stand it. I don't know how he ever got to be president."

"I guess he just wished himself there."

"That sounds too easy."

"It probably was."

"You haven't heard about all his scandals this year? The women he's paid off? Money issues and lies. I can't understand how he's still there."

"Nah. I don't keep up with it," Zoë said.

"You should. This foolishness is going to make history books. Little Honest will grow up reading about 45." I slid his pants up his thighs.

"I'll cross that bridge when I get there, but I wouldn't waste my time watching this. No offense."

"You should want to be in the know. It's good be aware of what's going on in this country."

"Aware is one thing, obsessed is another. A lot of people watch it, and then watch it again, and then find another video saying the same thing in a different way, or in a different voice, and watch that. And then they talk about it with whoever they can find. They want to know what other people's thoughts are on the topic in order to justify their own thoughts. And in the end—nothing. They've changed nothing, done nothing more than speculated, formed opinions, and gotten angry."

"Is that why you don't have a TV in your place?" I sat next to her and cradled Honest in my arms.

"No, that's not why. I don't watch it much, so I never bought one."

"I still think it's good to catch the news when it comes on."

"Why?"

"It's not good to be ignorant to what's going on."

"Ignorance is truly bliss," she said with a shrug.

"I don't see how."

"I'm not mad, for one. I don't think about the orange man in the toupee for hours on end. 99% of the things reported in the news have nothing to do with me. And the other 1% would be so serious that I'll catch it by some other means."

"Where'd you get that from?"

"I didn't get it from anywhere. I just don't see how knowing *everything* helps me. Do you know?" she asked.

I had to think about it for a moment. "The news can show you where our world needs help. If you don't know, how can you show up for other people?"

"Hmm. Was it on the news that your 21-year-old neighbor, who recently had a baby, didn't know what the hell she was doing and desperately needed help? Did your news source prompt you to walk next door to see about the crying baby?"

"No. Of course not."

"But here you are. You've shown up to help me. I believe we're guided to where we could be of service to other people."

"I understand that, but it's not—. It's just so small."

"So, an act of kindness must be major, groundbreaking, world-impacting to be noble and life-altering?" She crossed her arms. "I don't think you can tell that to a woman whose baby was starving before you intervened. What you did may never make headlines, but my gratitude is as great as the masses of people once starving in Ethiopia."

"That means a lot. It's good to be appreciated."

"I think we would rather find reasons to be aggravated and angry than appreciative. I'm not saying that injustices don't happen, but dwelling on them won't help anyone."

"Is that how you feel about the young people out here protesting when black boys are killed?"

"On some level, they're very organized. They're levelheaded and intentional. They have a purpose that's aligned with serving black people as a whole—like MLK or Malcolm X did before them. Those were voices created to reach the masses. But what were the names of the individuals who took part in sit-ins and boycotts, black or white? Or those who showed up to register to vote when they were at risk of being jailed, beaten or killed? The ones who didn't have a crowd behind them? Were they less brave or impactful?"

"To some degree, yes."

"Tell that to Jesus. His disciples weren't performing miracles. And he went to the cross alone, without any backup. Or what about Henrietta Lacks? The cancerous cells of a single woman have greatly impacted modern medicine."

"That's true, but there is still strength and power in numbers."

"Not when it comes to the things that matter most in this world."

"So, the boys being killed don't matter?"

"Yes, they do. Always. To ever feel your life doesn't matter is a great injustice, but it's an even greater injustice to spend a lifetime trying to convince others that you do instead of living out your truth. It's paralyzing, not productive. If my actions, my lifestyle, or the love I have for others, can't prove that my life matters, then you just can't be convinced. My words won't do better justice. Protestors know that. That's why peaceful protests turn to looting and property being destroyed. It's the result of people who have run out of words to say what their good actions and pure intent had already failed to prove, and they're frustrated. They're hurting because they're not understood, haven't been in all this time, and can't even force it."

"It's not easy to ignore what's going on and live your best

life. This stuff is everywhere."

"It's not. It's on your television screen, so you believe it's everywhere. How many black boys were killed here in Tallahassee?"

"Maybe not locally, but there were several in the state of Florida over the years. Before Trayvon Martin, there was Martin Lee Anthony in Panama City. That's close enough."

"Yeah, and in both cases, all of the perpetrators were acquitted. It's so hard to talk about this without sounding insensitive, but think of this: how many white boys have been killed for petty foolishness—drug deals, heated arguments, jealousy, ruthless women?"

"I don't know, but I know they're not getting shot by cops."

"White cops don't shoot white people?"

"Only after they've exhausted all other options. They don't give black boys a chance out here."

"You don't see headlines about white people killing other white people, right?"

"Not really—unless they're a celebrity, or infamous."

"Yet you hear about *black* boys who are killed unjustly?" she asked. "Or, you hear about black boys killing other black boys?"

"Yeah. It's everywhere."

"And the people who consistently tune in are being controlled in two ways. One, you learn that black people are constantly getting into trouble and killing each other. They're beasts, untrustworthy, out to steal whatever they can—even a life. And two, the media attempts to intimidate black people into inferiority by constantly displaying how easily blacks can be killed and the perpetrator get away with it. It doesn't matter how many video tapes of the incident we collect, or how many of us show up outside a courthouse during the trial of the accused, they still get off. These stories aren't blasted over the news because the media feels bad or seeks justice for black folks. They purposely display the pain and frustration to incite anger that no one can express in a way that would change their condition—maybe put a few black people in jail. For centuries, violence and bloodshed has been a tool used to control populations of people, especially during slavery. If we all acknowledge that disproportionate mass incarceration hasn't changed, and there are way too many black men in prison, why do we think other methods of domination and control has? Nah. Show me a Morehouse graduation ceremony, the histories of Eatonville, Florida or the Black Wall Street of Tulsa, Oklahoma or Durham, North Carolina, or the success of Marcus Garvey's economic strategies."

"Your solution is to just tune out all the bad?"

"I consciously guard my eye and ear gates. Sometimes we adopt what we see and hear as our truth, and sometimes what we're seeing is far from who we are."

"The televised march on Selma was a benefit to blacks, and it helped the Civil Rights movement."

"Still, it depicts the fight for equality. What shows blacks winning? We do win, right?"

"The 1968 Olympics. Tommie Smith and John Carlos were brave enough to stand for human rights during the Olympic ceremony."

"And so was Colin Kaepernick in 2016. They were all ostracized the same," Zoë said. "I don't want Honest to grow up watching the news and feeling discouraged, afraid, and pessimistic because it's shown him that he's disposable, or that he doesn't matter. Instead, I want him to know his strength, the power of his mind, the endless possibilities there are within him. It's less about tuning out, and more about tuning in to what I can do to help people—even the ones right next door. I'm not trying to build a resume of good deeds. I just want to be good to people."

~

Do you think Zoë's perspective made her likeable in a society where there has been a consistent divide?

If it did, or didn't, I don't think she cared. I found myself offended by some of the things she would say, but she spoke in a way for me to better understand *her* than to change my perspective. She went against the grain, but it wasn't attached to any cause. For instance, Christians will share what they believe to steer people in a certain direction. Or different political parties will convince you to believe one thing or another for votes, or to move a specific agenda. Zoë wasn't like that. Everything she spoke of was centered on the purity of her own heart and how she connected with other people. There was no agenda greater than that, it seemed. I think what is most baffling is the fact that a mindset like hers was developed in a woman not yet old enough to rent a car, and barely old enough to sip a glass of wine.

What was Zoë like having to juggle school and motherhood?

She didn't seem overwhelmed, or stressed. She managed everything well by my observation. She returned at the set time she said she would—-even stopped to grab something for me to eat on occasion. She was always pleasant. She would smile and say, "gimmee gimmee" every time she wanted me to hand Honest over to her. Honest was an addition to the life she already had—-not a burden.

She was a deeply happy person. The only time I saw her worried or frustrated was the night I went over to help with the baby's feeding. Even the things that should have knocked her down, didn't.

What things are you referring to?

I would say… in mid-to-late November, I saw a few disconnection notices from the power company on her door. And in December, I started to see notices from our landlord as well. I don't know what they said because they were sealed in envelopes, but I knew they weren't good. She was in high spirits before she took the notices from her door, and she was the exact same afterwards-- totally unbothered. I don't know if she had a plan to cover her expenses, but she wasn't working at the time.

When was the last time you saw Zoë?

The day she died, I went over to drop off one of Honest's bottles she had accidentally left at my place. She opened the door slowly, and held a finger in front of her mouth. I could see Honest sleeping in the corner of the sofa, and knew she wanted me to be quiet. I mouthed, "okay", and handed her the bottle. She smiled, and whispered, "Thank you."

I had already locked up my place, and was heading to my mother's house for the day. I went to that shack of a garage, and pulled my car out. I looked for passing traffic, and noticed a utility truck from the power company coming down the road. I wanted to make the turn out of the garage, but the truck slowed, and I couldn't determine when it would stop. Sure enough, he stopped in front of our duplex. I was finally able to pull out. I knew I had been late with that month's payment, but I was confident it had indeed been paid.

I watched the power guy from my rearview as he stuck something on Zoë's door, and after a moment, he was completely out of sight.

Did you ever think Zoë would kill herself?

She was strong for such a young lady. The strength and wisdom she had, I didn't have until I was over thirty and had to figure out how to manage six babies on my own after losing their father. Zoë had that almost ten times over. I couldn't have known.

If you could do anything differently in regards to your relationship with Zoë, what

would it be?

I don't know. I exhausted everything in my power to help her, just short of paying her bills. She never accepted anything more than help with Honest, but that wasn't the fullness of her needs. If she would have said something, I would have found help for her.

How did you learn of her death?

I found her--and Honest too.

EXHIBIT TWO: Zoë's Garage

Date: Thursday, January 16, 2020
Time: 6:56 PM
Location: Tallahassee, Florida

INTERVIEW NINE

Date: Friday, January 17, 2020
Time: 10:21 AM
Location: Tallahassee, Florida

SOURCE: OFFICER MARK HARMON

I received the call to head over to the scene at 10 a.m. on the morning of January 16th. The neighbor of the deceased had placed a 911 call around 9:45, and I was close to the area. She said she had recently returned home, parked her car in the garage, and was walking away when she heard music coming from the other side of the garage. She told the operator her neighbor wasn't answering the front door. She also mentioned having a hard time opening the garage on her own, but she could smell exhaust fumes, and it caused her to panic.

When I pulled up, the neighbor, a middle-aged woman, had taken refuge from the cold by staying inside her home. The morning started with 30-degree temperatures, and the climb from there was slow. I knocked on the woman's door, and she immediately came outside as if she had watched me approach from the window.

"Good morning, officer," she said, and bunched her housecoat tightly around her neck.

"Good morning. I'm responding to the call you placed a little while ago."

She nodded, anxious for assistance.

141

"Can you show me where the problem is?" I asked.

She pointed to a small, two-car garage on the other side of the street. "Let me put my shoes back on, and I can show you."

"No need, ma'am. It might be best that you stay right here."

"The girl who lives next door's name is Zoë. She didn't answer when I knocked, but I can hear music coming from her side of the garage over there."

"Okay. Let me check it out." The woman closed the door as I walked away, but I turned and noticed her watching from her window.

Approaching the garage, I could hear a very faint sound. Closer, I could make out the melody. There was music playing from inside. I slid my fingers along the bottom of the garage door to pull it open with a single hand, but somehow it was stuck. I placed both hands beneath the thick door, and used the weight of my body to pull with all my strength. It opened.

There was an old Camry parked inside, and the stench of gasoline escaped the space. Someone sat in its driver's seat, which was stretched back as far as it could go.

"Hello," I called out as I neared the vehicle, but the person didn't respond.

As I inched closer, and fearing the worst, I noticed a young, African American woman in a thick coat. There was a wadded blanket on her chest, and she appeared to be sleeping—or so I'd hoped. I tapped on the window. She didn't budge. I pulled the door handle and it opened.

"Ma'am," I said. No response.

Both of her hands were wrapped around the blanket on her chest. I moved her left hand and tried to read her pulse. There wasn't one. Something strange caught my attention. From the blanket on her chest, I could see what appeared to be the cheek and mouth of a doll. I lowered the blanket a little. It was a baby—a real one, and he too had expired. I backed out of the car and observed the two of them, sleeping peacefully. I've been on many gruesome scenes— from people who were nearly decapitated in car crashes to a homicide victim whose eye was shot clean from his face. Never had I seen anything like that girl and baby, and I was sick.

I walked out of the garage, placed the call, and I waited. The neighbor, in boots, the housecoat, and a thick jacket, came towards the scene.

"What's going on?" she asked. "That's her car in there."

"You should go back inside your house," I informed her.

"Why?" Panic set in. "She in there?" she asked, and the

warmth of her breath mingled with the cold, still air and created puffs of white smoke.

I gently grabbed the woman's shoulders and created a barrier between her and the scene, but she repeatedly maneuvered her body to look past me. She must have gotten a glimpse into the car because her next words were, "Oh no," and, shocked, she covered her mouth with her hands. For a moment, she was speechless and panting.

"Ma'am, go back inside," I told her.

"What happened to her? Zoë!" she yelled. "Officer, is she dead?"

Two officer cars pulled onto the scene, and blocked the roadway.

"Let me help you back inside," I said.

"No! Where's the baby?" she asked hysterically. "Where's Honest?" she shoved against my restraint.

"Go back inside," I demanded. "Please."

She let go and began to cry. A female officer rushed over to assist.

"Okay now," the officer said to the woman as she locked arms with her. "Let's get you inside where it's warm."

The third officer on the scene peeked at the bodies inside the car, and immediately returned to the garage's exterior.

"Hard to look at, isn't it?" I said to him, but he didn't respond.

The team of investigators arrived, and I was focused on sealing off the scene, but anxious to know what happened to the girl beyond what was obvious. I listened closely as they spoke in passing. They speculated that she had died of carbon monoxide poisoning, and they made note of the fact that her keys were still in the "on" position. Whatever gasoline she had in her car had been completely depleted at some point in the night, but the battery kept everything going—her phone charging, the music she played on the stereo. They had been deceased for only a few hours when they were discovered.

I completed my reports on the incident. After examination, the girl's toxicology screen showed that she had ingested oxycodone around the time of her death. For investigators, this incident was clearly suicide.

~

Did you see the bottle of pills Zoë used the day she died?

When we went into her home to thoroughly investigate, we found a nearly-full bottle of the drug in her bathroom. There only two tablets missing from it, but her name was indeed on the bottle. The prescription had been filled about three months before the incident.

If the prescription was filled 3 months earlier, why would she wait until then to take them?

That, I can't say, but it greatly supported the theory that she had taken her own life. Perhaps they were a numbing agent for her to go through with it. There are a lot of people who aren't sober at the time of a suicide attempt.

So, it wasn't possible for Zoë to think rationally after ingesting the drug?

Some users get accustomed to the effects of Oxys, but if you're typically sober and don't use medications regularly, it can definitely cause impairment. It can also impact someone's ability to make solid judgements.

Knowing that, do you believe it was her intent to end her life that night?

I can't say for sure, but there was more evidence at the scene that made me second-guess what I initially assumed happened to her.

What was that?

When we went inside her home, the power had been cut by the electric company. Without heat, she had to be cold the night before when the temperature almost touched 20 degrees. When inside her home, even with my coat on, and constantly moving around, I trembled like I was standing on the front lawn. It was freezing in there.

I considered the possibility of her going into the garage to keep warm in the car, and she took her child in there with her. Because she was on medication, she wasn't thinking clearly. From my perspective, it became more likely that the girl's death was an accident. My colleagues said the theory was just wishful thinking, and I wanted to believe them, but there were other clues.

Like what?

Her phone was plugged into the car's charger, which meant she planned to use it again; the knob that controls the heat was on high and in the "on" position, although nothing was blowing when we arrived; and there was an overnight bag stuffed with clothing for her and the baby inside the car. When we scanned her cell phone for calls made that evening, she had called two shelters. I contacted them personally, and discovered that on the evening she died, both facilities were full. It proves that she tried to find better conditions for herself and the baby.

That's not it. The strongest evidence in my defense was the baby resting on her chest. I've known women to kill their children. And none of them are affectionately cradling them when they do it. But whatever, I could be completely wrong. Wishful thinking.

Even with your "wishful thinking", that's enough connected dots to know that this woman didn't kill herself.

Maybe. But what could I do about it? The case was closed before her body reached the morgue.

Why couldn't they see what you saw in this whole situation?

I don't know, but it wasn't my job to make them see it. I was the responding officer. That's it. When the higher-ups say, "it's done", it's done. However, when it came to this incident, I admit I got wrapped up and was way too invested in knowing what happened to her. I had never seen anything like that before.

And you're saying the others weren't as invested?

I can't speak for the others. All officers of the law are drawn to certain incidents for various reasons. This one drew me in. I have a younger sister in New York about the same age as Zoë was. She's in college too. I must have imagined for a moment that this girl could have been my baby sister. I wanted to know more about the incident, but it didn't anger me when the others didn't have the same level of interest in her. For some of us, it's just a job.

But you acknowledge there was more to it than they were looking for?

Yes. I do. Listen. I wasn't going to mention this, but I followed up on a few things--just out of curiosity. The doctor listed on the prescription bottle was a local OBGYN. Based on the date it was filled, she received it after the birth of her baby. I visited the doctor who prescribed the Oxys. When my wife had our children, doctors wouldn't give her anything stronger than ibuprofen--even when she asked--so I didn't know why Zoë would receive something so potent.

The doctor told me that Zoë had some complications during the delivery, but wouldn't tell me what they were. Even more interesting, when the doctor recommended that Zoë get the prescription for the Oxys filled, Zoë refused the prescription. As a result, the doctor requested it be filled at the hospital's pharmacy, and had a nurse hand it to her before she was released. Whatever the condition was, Zoë's doctor expected a painful recovery.

Did you dig into Zoë's history? Were there any complaints made by, or against, her that would raise eyebrows?

No. Nothing. She was a student in a college town, but she didn't get into trouble with the law--no public intoxication or speeding tickets.

Was there any inquiry made into people she may have been in relationships with, or friends?

147

No. Once her death was considered a suicide, there was nothing more for anyone to do. We sent officials to make contact with a relative in Miami, but that was it. The police department must be mindful of how we use our resources. It's not always easy to walk away from a case like Zoë's, but we don't have a choice. We move on to help others who still need our help.

May I see the images you brought with you?

Sure. It wouldn't have been appropriate to show you images of the scene inside the garage, but I brought a few shots from inside her place. I thought sharing these could help you see how she lived before she perished. Her place was clean. There were a few baby items here and there, but it appears she kept everything neat. There were school books under her bed and stacked in her closet.

I see. Do college bookstores still have the buyback option?

To my knowledge, they do.

Hmm. I wonder why she didn't sell these books. In these pictures, it looks like she's hoarding them.

Well, collectively, they may be worth something, but individually, she wouldn't have gotten much for them. A trip to a burger joint could spend it easily. These kids spend hundreds on books, and when they sell them back, they're only worth nickels.

These candles—-in the picture—-can you recall the brand?

Umm…I think they were called "Lit". It was cold in her apartment, so I couldn't tell for sure if they had been burned in that timeframe. To have a newborn, who usually stinks up a place as small as hers with soiled diapers and soaked towels of spit-up, her apartment smelled nice--tropical. I remember picking up one of the candles in the picture, and it was fairly new. She had probably only used it once.

Why? Do you own some of these?

No, I don't. But I know someone who does.

Interview Ten
(FOLLOW-UP)

Date: Friday, January 17, 2020
Time: 1:23 PM
Location: Tallahassee, Florida

SOURCE: MARIE DOBSON

I need you to be truthful with me. Did you see Zoë after the night in the mall?

Yes. Travis and I both did--in late January; the day she died. She wasn't the girl I had seen through the store window or at the bar sipping on ginger ale. And she didn't smile.

~

  It was almost 8 at night, and Travis and I had just come in from dinner. Since we decided to stay in our marriage, he made great effort, and was consistent with taking me out on dates. That Tuesday in January was one of them.
  It was extremely cold that night. While it was hard to be sexy with so many layers, I made it work with a red, fitting, knee-length dress, black pumps, and a thick coat that stopped mid-calf. I

went into our bedroom to undress for the second half of our date when there was a knock at the front door. Moments later, I heard the doorbell. Travis was already in the kitchen pouring glasses of wine for our nightcap, so I trusted he would answer. I had only taken off my shoes and coat when I heard Zoë's voice.

I walked barefoot against the cold, hardwood floor into the living room, and she stood there—holding a baby carrier covered by a pale-yellow blanket.

"What is she doing here?" I asked Travis.

"I don't know." He closed and locked the door. "What's going on, Zoë?" he asked.

I could tell by the expression on her face that our home was the last place she'd desired to be. It was sad, and weighed heavily with humility.

"I didn't come to bother you, but I need some help," she said as she looked to each of us.

"With what, Zoë?" Travis asked.

"It's dark, and it's cold, and I don't have any power at my place."

"You trying to stay the night? No. We're not doing that around here," I said firmly.

"Wait a minute, Marie," Travis said, and held up his hand to silence me. He looked down at the baby carrier. "What's that?"

"The baby," Zoë said. "I think he's still asleep from the ride over here."

"You had a baby?" Travis asked her.

She looked in my direction, and then back to him. "She didn't tell you?"

"Who?" He pointed towards me. "Marie?"

"I had our baby on October 5th." She looked at the covered carrier. "His name is Honest."

Travis looked directly at me. "What? You knew about this?" he asked hysterically.

I couldn't find the words to say to him, so I stood there and stared at them.

"I'll take that as a 'yes'." He moved like gelatin to a seat on the sofa.

Zoë placed the baby's carrier on the floor to relieve herself of the weight, but she didn't invite herself into our living space. She stood there and tucked her hands into her coat pockets.

I wanted to comfort Travis, or at least minimize the blow of my deception. "Why would I tell you what I didn't know for sure? That baby could be anybody's."

"I was up front with you—about everything. Are ya'll serious right now?" He turned to look back at Zoë.

He watched her mouth as she uttered an innocent "I'm sorry," and then he slouched back into his seat.

"You're not going to believe her, are you?" I said desperately as I sat next to him.

"Give me a minute to sort through all this. Just give me a minute." He balled his fist and pressed it against his mouth.

Zoë seemed to regret barging in on us the way she had because she lifted the carrier from the floor and maneuvered herself to leave.

"I shouldn't have done this," she said, and started towards the door.

"Don't," Travis' stern voice stopped her. He stood from the sofa and went towards her. "You said you don't have any power. It's only 30-something degrees out there." He looked at me before his next statement, and then said in a lowered voice, "The walls are thin at your place, Zoë. It gotta be cold in there."

Offense bubbled up within me like shaken Coke. "You will not offer her a goddam thing, Travis," I commanded.

I got up from my seat and stormed into her space. She nervously took a step backwards with the baby carrier locked securely in her grip.

"What about the *other* guy?" I said to her.

"What?" she asked, puzzled.

"What about the man who puts his hands on you? The one who beats you?"

Travis, also bewildered, turned to me and said, "What the hell are you talking about, Marie?"

"What other guy?" Zoë asked.

"She's in an abusive relationship, Travis." I looked at her as scornfully as my facial features would permit. "I saw you there—in the group counseling session for battered women. I followed you. You couldn't have been more than five or six months pregnant then." I looked back to my husband and pointed at the carrier. "This baby must be his."

Zoë didn't speak a single word.

I continued with disgust, "And here you are trying to pin a baby on a decent, hardworking man. But he's mine, and I won't stand for it."

Zoë turned to leave.

"What you said at the bar was bullshit. I see you actually do care what people think of you," I taunted her.

153

"Zoë, wait a minute," Travis called out.

"No! Let her leave. She knows I'm telling the truth."

"You shouldn't fix your mouth to say things you have no understanding of," Zoë said, and then she was gone.

I could sense that Travis wanted to run after her, so I intentionally planted a seed that stopped him in his tracks. "Why do you think she didn't tell you? Travis, the baby is not yours. Don't be fooled by this girl. She will figure it out," I said as he watched her get into her car and drive away.

Zoë never removed the blanket. And Travis never saw the baby's face.

~

And that's it?

That's it.

Look at this picture. It's the one I took at the end of your interview the other day. Look at the candles burning behind you.

Okay. And?

Now look at this one. These are the same candles in Zoë's home—-fairly new—-when her body was discovered. Considering the financial strain Zoë faced, how could she afford these? They're not sold in stores, but shipped from New York. Did you see Zoë again after she came to your home the night she died?

Let's say--a scorned wife grows weary of this pest of a woman who's looking for whatever handout she could find. The wife goes over to the woman's place, dopes her, places her in a parked car in a garage, cranks it up, and then seals the garage.

Okay. Keep going.

I'm sure there are women who could do something like that to someone. I won't deny thinking about various methods myself, especially after the hurt my husband felt when he learned about the baby. Oh, how devastated he was when he tried to call her a few days later and her mother, who had her phone, gave him news that Zoë and the baby were dead. It broke me to see him in so much pain. Do you know what it's like to stand by and watch the person you love most in this world mourn the loss of his ex-lover, and a baby you don't share with him? You can't imagine what it feels like, so don't judge me for contemplating what it would be like to make her go away—-to fully win my husband back.

But that scenario just isn't true. It is not what happened. In your imagined soap opera, I'm some villainous creature set out to destroy this girl, but the opposite was true. She broke her word to never tell Travis about the baby when I was ready to move on.

Yes, I went to Zoë's place after she left our home that night, but only for a few minutes. Travis was called into the office an hour or so after she left, and I began to feel sorry for how I'd handled her. I packed some candles I'd purchased online the week before, and I took them over to her.

~

It was after 10 p.m. when I arrived at the apartment I'd followed Zoë to a few months earlier. Everything was dark and silent—even her neighbor's home. She opened the door after I knocked, and seemed completely zoned out. It was like she hadn't slept in days. I was so infuriated by the fact that she had come to my home and unleashed my deception that I didn't notice her condition

155

before.

"Can I come in?" I asked.

She stuffed her hands into her coat pocket and shivered. "Why? What do you want?"

"I brought a few candles to help get you through the night."

She looked back into her apartment, and then at me, before opening the door for me to come inside. The apartment was minimally lit. She had only three candles spread over the living room area. I went straight to her kitchen, which overlooked the living room, and removed the six candles from the bag I carried. I used a lighter that was resting on the countertop to ignite them. With her hands stuffed into her coat, she stood on the other side of the counter and watched. Her phone rang in her pocket. She took it out to look at it, and then put it back.

I made my way out of the kitchen, and folded the bag.

"Thank you," she said.

"No problem."

I was about to leave, but I saw the baby resting on a pillow on the floor. He was fully clothed, and had a thick pair of socks on his feet; he wore another pair on his hands like mittens. He made little noises and swatted playfully at the air with his sock-covered hands. Zoë caught me staring, and asked if I wanted to hold him.

"No," I said. "I shouldn't."

"He's a good baby." She looked at him endearingly.

I couldn't bring myself to do it. Zoë grabbed the top of her head, and moaned in pain.

"You okay?" I asked her.

"My head is bothering me, but I'll be fine. Thank you again for the candles."

"Do you have something to take?" I asked her.

"I don't know. I don't think so." She wobbled as though she was about to pass out.

"Sit down on the sofa," I told her. "Do you mind if I look to see if you have anything in there?"

She laid her head against the arm of the sofa. "Sure."

Her phone rang again, and she placed it next to her.

I grabbed a candle for light, went to her bathroom and checked all over. There weren't any over-the-counter pain relievers, but I came across a prescription bottle with her name on it—dated in October of the previous year. The girl must have had a Cesarean, or some serious health issues, because the pills in the bottle were Oxys. I grabbed two, and went into the living room to hand them to her. She was reluctant to take them from me, but I told her that she could get some rest and that her headache would be gone.

She took them from my hand and walked into the kitchen for water. Her phone lit up and vibrated on the couch. I was curious, and wanted to know who had been calling, but Zoë could see me from her position in the kitchen. The phone went dark, and immediately lit up again. I moved closer and glanced down at it quickly. I was instantly relieved to know the caller was not my husband, and that he hadn't snuck off to connect with her.

"I'll go now," I said.

She looked at me over the rim of the glass as she drank. She lowered it from her face and said, "Goodnight."

That was it. I left her and the baby there—alive.

~

I can't believe that.

Why is it so hard to believe? Perhaps it went like this: I give her the candles and I leave; she possibly wakes up lethargic, grabs her baby, goes outside to her parked car in the garage, comforts the baby on her chest, and then cranks it up. It seems reasonable to me.

Wait. How did you know that?

Know what?

How did you know where Honest was in the car?

News articles, I think.

How he was positioned in the car was never made public.

I mean, where else would he be?

The passenger seat, or lying on the backseat

somewhere--the trunk even.

You know--I don't understand why I'm a suspect in your fantasy files, but if you should check out anyone, it's her friend.

Why?

While I was at Zoë's place, someone was blowing up her phone, but she kept sending the calls to voicemail until she finally turned off the ringer and put it on vibrate. Of course, I wondered if it was my husband. It wasn't, but I also considered it could be some other guy she was involved with-- especially the one who had her in those victims' meetings. When the phone was on the sofa, and she went to get water for the Oxys, I looked. The caller had attempted twice in less than two minutes.

The phone's ID read: "My ♥ Destiny".

INTERVIEW ELEVEN

(FOLLOW-UP)

Date: Friday, January 17, 2020
Time: 4:44 PM
Location: Tallahassee, Florida

SOURCE: DESTINY WILLIAMS

I have a few additional questions for you, if you don't mind. Are you ready to get started?

Yes, but first I want to go on record and clarify something.

What's that?

I won't pretend you didn't just see Marcus leave here. And I'm sure you saw us kissing too.

How long have you been seeing Zoë's ex-boyfriend?

They were never officially in a relationship. Zoë would have told you that herself. They were friends. To answer your question: Marcus and I didn't connect until after the ceremony we attended for Zoë. The relationship between us didn't start until a few months after she was gone. He and I kept in touch, and we would reminisce about her. It felt good to share our past experiences being with Zoë, and it brought us closer.

What kind of relationship would you say you have with Marcus?

We are what we are. Friends, or lovers when we wanna be. It looks promising though.

And so do his chances of being drafted in June.

What is that supposed to mean?

Nothing. I don't mean to overstep boundaries. I want to get to the point of my visit. Were you angry with Zoë the night she died?

No. Why would you ask that?

You called her repeatedly that night, and she didn't answer your calls. Were you harassing her?

No. I didn't harass her. And I wasn't angry with her either. It was the other way around. Zoë had distanced herself from me.

Did it have anything to do with Marcus?

No. I told you already. Marcus and I didn't
link up until after Zoë died. Zoë was hurt,
but it had nothing to do with a man.

~

I didn't return to State at the start of spring semester. I was back in Tampa, Florida, my hometown, and had been there since the previous summer. At the time, I had been in an off and on relationship with a guy I'd known since high school. If Tampa was where he was, it was where I wanted to be. It was only a few months earlier that Zoë comforted me after aborting the baby he and I created, but I was still hooked on him. My love for him had enormous power—one that made aborting babies and abandoning responsibilities easy.

I called on occasion to chat with Zoë during my time away but, near the end, I could tell Zoë didn't like to talk about my guy friend. She would never say it, but I noticed how she would grow incredibly quiet and just let me talk. When I was all done ranting about my lack of trust in him, or suspicions about other girls, she would start on a totally different topic.

My relationship with him wasn't the only reason I jumped ship and hadn't returned to Tallahassee. After the abortion procedure in July, I had some spotting on the first day; but by the second day, it had become heavier than the day before. With the bleeding, came a pain in my abdomen like I've never experienced. I shivered, but was drenched in sweat throughout the night. I hoped the symptoms would pass, but they didn't.

I visited one of those quick clinics, and when they asked about my activities that week, I told them about the abortion. They immediately referred me to my gynecologist, whose office was back in Tampa. I popped some ibuprofen, got a Greyhound ticket, and confessed my recent acts to my mother as I took the slow bus ride to Tampa.

The following morning, I was in emergency surgery to repair the damage of a terribly perforated uterus. I was in an unhealthy relationship; had recently aborted my baby; and, just my luck, I found out the doctor fucked me up during the procedure. One of the instruments had pierced straight through my uterus.

I wasn't in the right headspace to return to school that fall, so I didn't make plans to go back. Newly twenty-one, I started to drink excessively, while convincing my mom that I needed only a single semester to feel good enough to get back into the swing of college. Before I knew it, it was mid-January and I had re-occupied my childhood bedroom for an entire six months. I was so sick of *me*—disappointed, discouraged, and completely down on myself—so I got drunk.

I always pick the shittiest times to say the wrong things, and I drunk-dialed Zoë two days before she died. My intention was to catch up with her like I had done at least once a week since we had been apart, but the conversation took off in a direction I never expected. Of course, I nearly filled the time with my guy troubles, and she discussed how she needed an additional semester to graduate, and wouldn't be finished until December. She sounded like her old self, but with a *new* plan.

"The way I see it, I'll start a new career in a new city at the top of the new year," Zoë said excitedly. "So clutch."

"Yeah. Right," I said.

Something in me didn't want to be happy for her; and nothing in me acknowledged the sacrifice of two semesters she'd made to have the baby. Zoë's victory was nowhere near, but her optimism was sickening.

"When are you coming back? You still want to finish up here, right?" she asked. I could hear the baby make little screeching noises in the background. She must have pulled him up towards her shoulder because the sound seemed closer, and louder.

I took a big gulp of cheap, peach-flavored rum right from the bottle. By that point, it was over half-empty, and I was lit. "I'll be there when I get there," I said.

"You think you'll finish in December too?" she pressed.

"Damn!" I snapped. "Maybe I don't wanna come back to Tallahassee."

Given our history, Zoë knew immediately that something was wrong. "You wanna tell me what's going on with you, or nah?" she asked.

The baby made a short, screeching sound like he was about to cry.

"Shh," she calmly said to him.

"Why did you let me do it, Zoë?" I asked, and took another swig from the bottle.

"Huh? Honest is trying to fuss at me. What did you say?"

"How could a true friend let me do something like this to myself?" There it was. She was the scapegoat for my generously fucked up position.

"Are you serious right now?" she asked.

"Yeah, Zoë. You wanna see my life fucked up like yours,

don't you? You let me go to that cheap ass clinic, and you didn't say shit. You just let me do it."

The chaos-creating blend of regret and liquor caused me to weep. Zoë was silent, but I knew she was still on the other end of the line because I could hear Honest very clearly.

"And there you are with a baby by a man who didn't want your ass." I lifted the bottle to my mouth again and sucked it down. "What? You jealous?" I laughed. "I don't have a plan to fix all my shit, but you're still jealous. I can come back to school whenever the fuck I want—and with no baby. Jealous, right?" Another gulp.

I poured every ounce of my frustration out on her, and more liquor into my mouth. I was beyond faded, so I can't recall what else I said that night, or how the conversation ended, but I don't recall hearing Zoë's voice after my initial insult.

The following morning, I awoke with my arm wrapped around the base of the toilet. Being sick hindered me from immediately remembering the previous night's events, but I thought about Zoë. And without any recollection of the foul shit I'd said to her, I wished she was there to hold back my hair as I puked up my guts as she had done so many times before. This time, she wasn't there.

When I sobered up that afternoon, memories from the night before came flooding in, and I called her. No answer. I tried again, and again, and again. I can't guess how many times I pressed the "call" button above her name. I played back the conversation repeatedly, and I knew it was bullshit. I desperately wanted to apologize, to make things right with her, but when Zoë was hurt or tired of talking to brick walls, she removed herself. For her, it was protection from negative energy; but for me, it was punishment.

I called her restlessly over the next four days. When I learned that Zoë would never answer my calls again, she had already been gone for two days.

~

What were your thoughts once you discovered what happened to Zoë?

I was numb for a while. I thought what I'd said to her provoked her to do it. No one could tell me it didn't. There wasn't a note, a message, or a clue about what Zoë felt the day she died, but I knew she wasn't answering my calls. I felt responsible.

Do you still feel that way?

Sometimes, but I have more peace about it
now. I still don't know the details of Zoë's
final days, or what it was like for her; but
after I spent time reflecting on the type of
person she was--how tough, resilient, and
"no-fucks-given" she was--I can't believe
she would have let my bullshit drive her to
that point. It took some time to get here.

**It seems this *deep, undying* love you claim
to have had for Zoë never served her—-just
you.**

Are you saying I didn't love Zoë? I did. I
promise. At least, I loved Zoë the best I
knew how. The truth is that I couldn't meet
the mark, even when she was patient with me.
Yes, I was always wrapped up in my own
issues; and I admit, Zoë deserved a better
friend, but I won't let you tell me I didn't
love her.

**If you could do things all over again, would
you?**

Are you fuckin' serious? Yeah. I wouldn't
just erase what happened the night I got
drunk and hurt her. That wouldn't be enough.
I would go all the way back to the day we
met in our freshman dorm room. I would open
myself up enough to learn to be the friend
she had always been to me.

**One last question: Do you know if Zoë dated
someone who abused her?**

No. Who told you that? She never mentioned it to me. Zoë wasn't the type to stay in a situation if she was being abused on *any* level.

CHRISTINE RACHEAL

INTERVIEW TWELVE

Date: Saturday, January 18, 2020
Time: 2:01 PM
Location: Miami, Florida

SOURCE: GAYLE OLIVER

I lost my right leg at the scene when I was ejected from my parents' car. It was the summer of 1967, and I was eight years old when my father collided with a short, cement wall that divided the highway's exit from flowing traffic. He was distracted by another driver he'd cut off a few miles earlier, and didn't notice how the car crawled towards the shoulder of the road. He yelled at the passing driver, and gestured as aggressively as he could from his seat to win the battle against a careless stranger on a fast-moving freeway.

I was in the front seat. It was a treat my father would give me when no one else was with us. Although the seatbelt was secured across my lap, upon impact, I flew quickly through the windshield of the car and was tossed onto the cement wall before I fell onto the pavement like a ragdoll. My right leg was left at the scene—somewhere between the shattered windshield and the hood of the car—when I was bused to the emergency room for life-saving surgery.

When I finally awoke, I was without my left leg too. A large bandage covered a wound so deep that it left a scar that stretched from ear to mouth. Patches of hair were completely gone, and

167

stitches kept my scalp intact—over 80 of them. My jaw was fractured; one of my collar bones was broken, along with three of my ribs; I lost three teeth, and my right arm had been fractured in two places. I spent nearly three months at the same hospital room, in the same bed, surrounded by the same people, with their same sympathetic sighs, but I was totally changed.

My father was angry at the audacity of the driver on the road that day, but his shame and frustration lasted the rest of his days as he was forced to watch his only daughter grow up badly disfigured. He would look at me with so much pity, it seemed that each day brought a new apology. I desired for him to have joy, and to delight in my presence again, so I did what I could and learned to care for myself. I learned to lift out of my wheelchair onto the toilet, or into a bath, to prepare food in the kitchen, and so forth. No matter what I achieved, he always looked at me with hope-drained eyes.

I was the poster child for growing up with limitations and conditions, which I had absolutely no control over. It wasn't until my thirties that I learned to live, and to love life. I had all control over how I responded to what life threw at me—total control over how I felt—about everything. I spent a decade exploring life beyond the home my parents left for me. I graduated college, travelled a little. After fully discovering who I was, and years of practice to maintain a perpetual state of bliss, I wanted to help someone else to find it for themselves. One day, I did.

Zoë was my first foster child. The social worker, upon dropping her off, shared only a few details of Zoë's childhood with me. The facts were gruesome, and she was only 11 years old. Initially, I feared the weight of taking someone like Zoë into my home, but I mustered the courage to trust that I could do it.

On her first day here, she just sat in the room I had prepared for her. She didn't eat or drink anything. As the sun went down, she didn't bother to turn on a lamp. As I passed her room an eighth time, I saw her sitting on the bed in only enough light to make out the edges of the room's furnishings, and I stopped to talk to her.

"Are you okay?" I asked.

"Yeah." She hung her head as she spoke, and seemed afraid to look at me.

"Do you want to turn on a light? It's dark in here."

"No."

"Do you want anything to eat? I have some beef, rice and vegetables in the kitchen. Or something else—anything in there, you can have. A sandwich? I have peanut butter and bananas."

"No, thank you," she said.

"Well, do you want a bath? It'll help you sleep better. Let me get you a towel."

I moved into the hallway and grabbed a towel from the low-standing shelf in the linen closet. After handing it to her, she began to shuffle through the clothes in her bag. The stench was horrible. The clothes were mildewed, but the smell didn't alarm Zoë. She was used to the odor.

"I have some clean t-shirts in my room. I washed them today. Maybe you can sleep in one of them tonight," I suggested.

"I have something," she said.

"Why don't you let me wash those." I moved my chair closer to her and reached for the bag as it sat on the bed.

"No!" she yelled, and pulled the bag tightly to her chest.

I backed away to give her some space. It was impossible to understand what she felt, but I understood she needed a moment to feel it completely.

"Those are your belongings. I know. I won't keep them from you. I promise. But I want you to be comfortable. And I want to properly clean your clothes."

She sat on the bed and continued to hold firmly to the bag.

"Will you let me?" I asked her. "Please."

I saw her fingers loosen, and slowly, the bag shifted away from her. She handed it over to me; I placed it on my lap, and backed out into the hallway. "I'll wash them right now, and give them back to you. You can wait until these things are dry before you take a bath if you'd like."

She sat there as if I had stripped her of everything she owned. If I had, it wasn't much at all.

After an hour or so, I placed the fresh stack of folded laundry on her bed and left her alone again. I heard water running into the bathtub, and then it stopped. I went into the hallway to check on her, but my concern was met with loud sobbing and the occasional sound of splashing water. I didn't bother her for the remainder of the evening.

When Zoë came here, she had nothing to connect her to the life she knew, or the people she loved. For weeks, it was like watching someone endure withdrawals in drug rehab. I had to spoon-feed normalcy to her. Her words were so few that, if I could string them together, they would only produce a fraction of a sentence.

Each day, I asked permission to help her—to make her food or prepare her clothes. I would emphasize that she could only let me help her *that day*; and if she didn't want me to help her the next day, it was okay. One thing was certain: I would never look at her with pity and sorrow the way my father had looked at me. I found an opportunity to call her "brave" or "strong" or "courageous" or "smart" each day.

After a few weeks, I could help her without asking. She understood that I was fine with moving at her pace, and taking it one day at a time. I wanted her to know that she didn't have any responsibility to me—I wouldn't force her to connect with me on some greater level if she wasn't ready. "Let's just get through the day," I would say. Besides, as a foster parent, I wasn't certain what the next day would bring.

Eventually, Zoë let me in completely but, in that process, she learned that people can interact and benefit from each other without permanent attachments. As a result, she became very detached.

~

Is there anything more you can tell me about Zoë's life before she came to live here?

Zoë experienced deep poverty--the kind that could ruin the mindset of generations. She and her sister, Daloris, were sent to live with their mother's cousin, Juby, when her mother was killed. Juby abandoned them after a number of years--just left them there. Child Protective Services received an anonymous tip that minors had been left in a home alone, and the girls were picked up.

Juby had children of her own, but a crack addiction really took her away from them. They were troublemakers, didn't go to school, and no one cared. Zoë told me about Juby's daughter, Lena, who was a little older than Daloris. She's the one who taught Daloris to turn tricks.

I don't recall Daloris sharing that with me.

Why would she? I think she tried to rid

herself of anything that reminded her—
including Zoë. I don't blame her. The one
person who couldn't forget seeing her come
and go with random men at Juby's home was
Zoë.

Zoë's heart broke for her sister. When she
came to live with me, it wasn't for her
parents that Zoë cried each night. She wanted
her sister; the one consistent relationship
she'd had her entire life. She was never
without Daloris before that. Even when her
mother died, and her father was in prison,
she had Daloris. Daloris was a smart girl.
She stayed in school regardless of their
circumstances, and graduated high school
soon after they were split up.

**Did you know where Daloris was placed after
the girls entered foster care?**

Yes. Child Protective Services gave me a
phone number and address for the family.

Did you ever take Zoë over for visits?

I tried a few times in the beginning. Each
time, they would tell me that Daloris was in
school, or that she was working some fast
food job and wouldn't be around. I spoke with
her myself one day, and she gave me the same
excuse.

**Was Zoë aware of your attempts to connect
her and her sister?**

Yes, of course. She desperately wanted to
see Daloris, and asked me to contact them
for her. I told her Daloris was busy with

school and work, which had been relayed to
me, but I spared her my own thoughts on the
matter. I didn't understand why Daloris was
so resistant to the idea of at least seeing
her sister until Zoë opened up about how ugly
their experiences together had been. It
started to make sense.

Did Daloris ever visit Zoë?

She came over once.

What was it like when she visited?

Interesting, and brief, to say the least.

~

I had grown accustomed to stares over the years. If
someone stares at your nose instead of your eyes, you assume there's
something hanging there. You'll turn away, or quickly swipe at your
nose and hope it's no longer there. For me, what caused people to
stare couldn't be flicked off or wiped away. Ironically, the part of my
face that was most intact, and normal—my eyes—were always
avoided. I learned to see past their drilling stares, reach within them
to grasp the innocence of their curiosity, and accept their
unfamiliarity.

I mastered being okay. My skin had become as tough as a
canvas sack, but children who didn't know any better would point,
and ask their parents what was wrong with the lady in the chair.
Although I wanted to, I couldn't smile. The scar across my face
would rise higher and bunch up near my eye—a scarier sight. People
were generally well-meaning, and their gawks were easy for me to
move past, but I can't say the same for Zoë.

It was her third week at home, and she was finally coming
out of her bedroom and into the living quarters with me. There is a
television in the living room. Zoë had the option to watch it if she
wanted; but she said Juby's home didn't have a working television,
and she didn't know what was good to watch. I didn't pressure her
to find a new, favorite television show. Instead, I pulled out old
board games, and puzzles, and books—anything that would keep

her entertained.

Zoë sat at the dining room table one evening and put together a jigsaw puzzle of a bird perched on a branch when I passed her in my chair.

"Can I ask you something?" she said.

"Sure." I moved closer to the table.

"How did you get like that?"

"In this chair? These scars?"

She nodded her head.

"I was in an accident when I was a little younger than you are now. I went through the car's windshield."

"Did it hurt?" she asked.

"I can't remember," I told her.

She went for a puzzle piece on the table and added it to the growing image.

"I bet it's good you don't remember," she said.

"And I bet you're right. Pain remembered is possibly just as bad as pain felt in the moment. The good thing is that when you survive it, and heal, hindsight reveals just how strong you really are."

"Does your face hurt?" she asked innocently.

"It's just a scar." I lifted a puzzle piece and added it. "Do you have any scars?"

"Just one," she said.

"Does it still hurt?"

"No."

"Do you remember when it hurt?"

"Yes. I do," she said.

"It's healed now. I'm sure it's much better, and you don't feel what it was like the day you got it."

"I guess," she shrugged as she moved another puzzle piece.

"Do you want to touch it?"

She looked over at me. "Your scar?"

"Yes."

She slowly nodded her head, and then turned towards me. Zoë extended her hand and pressed lightly against my skin.

"Are you afraid?"

"No." Her fingers swept gently across my face.

"Do you think I'm ugly?" I asked.

"I can tell you're pretty. You just have this scar. It's not so pretty though," she said honestly.

"Some people can hide their ugly; some people can't, but beneath it all is something beautiful. You can accept people's scars as a part of who they are—a part of their journey. You can ignore their scars and pretend they don't exist and miss out on a part of them that makes them who they are. Or you can more deeply embrace them because of it. That one isn't so easy, but if you can learn to do it, you have discovered what it means to love. Love isn't pity, or fear, or avoiding the truth, or getting rid of the whole person because of their speck of ugly."

"Did that happen to you?"

"Yes. A lot. That's why I know better."

She went back to her puzzle.

"Some bad things happened to you too. And one day, you'll use it to make yourself, and other people, better."

She didn't respond. She simply moved another piece from the end of the table into its proper place.

One Saturday, we were low on food and I needed to go out for groceries. I make use of the public transportation service to run errands, or for doctor's visits, and this day was no different. I called and requested a pickup for a trip to a nearby supermarket. Zoë was old enough to stay at home alone, but up to that point, she had never been here without me. I told her to get dressed for a little shopping.

The driver picked us up and whisked us off to a store about six miles away. Zoë helped by getting a shopping cart for the items, and was excited to push it through the market.

We started with produce, and she bagged a few tomatoes, a cabbage, onions, apples, bananas, and oranges. She delightfully placed them into the cart. I remained close, and instructed her to grab some poultry, a few cuts of beef, and a bag of frozen seafood.

"Come here," I said, and pulled a sanitizer wipe from the store's supply in the meat section. "Give me your hands."

"What's this for?"

As I wiped her hands, I told her, "Meat has bacteria. There could be some outside the packaging, and I don't want you to put it near your face."

"Can I get sick?"

"Only what you believe can make you sick, will. Let's take precaution just to stay clean."

She fanned her hands dry as a woman and her two children, boys around Zoë's age, came onto the aisle. I was ready to pick up a few condiments—some ketchup and mustard, maybe a bottle of ranch dressing—and I didn't notice as the blanket covering my lower extremities was falling to the floor. Beneath the blanket, I typically wear shorts with an elastic band. It's the most comfortable attire for a woman in my condition.

"Come on. Let's go down here," I instructed Zoë.

She shifted the cart towards the aisle, and it caught the bottom of the blanket, exposing the stomps and scars where my legs should have been. The boys saw, and made it known.

"Dang! Ma, she ain't got no legs," one of the boys said loudly as he tapped his mother.

Zoë noticed my freakishly deformed lower region, which she had not seen before, and quickly grabbed the blanket from the germy market floor and laid it over my lap.

"Look at her face, Mama," the other boy said.

"Come on here," their mother called.

I thought she would correct their behavior—point out how rude it is to talk about strangers in their presence. What she said next was, "God will get you if you ain't right. You can't run from His punishment, boys. And I wonder what that girl doing with her."

"Her mama white?" the youngest boy asked his mother.

"I don't know, chile. Come on."

Zoë heard each of their remarks as we passed the family on the aisle; she silently choked on them, and found them difficult to digest.

Zoë's response bothered me more than what caused it. She never had much of a poker face. When she was bothered by something, those around her knew it. She was no longer my excited grocery helper. She placed my requested items into the basket at a slower pace, and didn't look in my direction. Shame had come over her.

When we arrived home, and began to put away the groceries, I knew I had to talk to Zoë about what happened. She hadn't spoken the entire ride back, and I didn't want her to retreat to her bedroom and avoid me, which would be a backwards step.

"Do you want to talk?" I asked.

"Okay." She placed a box of cereal into the pantry.

"What happened at the market?"

"Nothing."

"You changed. You were sad."

She went to unload another plastic bag of food items. "I heard those people."

"What did it make you feel?"

"I don't know—bad."

"For who?" I asked.

"You."

"Why?"

"Because they said God did that to you."

"What do you know about God, Zoë?"

175

"He wants us to do good. He's everywhere. He created us."

"Do you know that God loves us?"

"Yes. That too."

"Do you believe He did this to me?"

"I don't know." She stopped manipulating the bags and faced me. "The lady in the store said he was punishing you. Is He? What did you do for Him to do that to you?"

"I was eight years old when I lost my legs. I was younger than you are, Zoë. What could I have done to God that He would punish me by taking my legs?"

"I don't know."

"God didn't take my legs, Zoë. The car accident did—anger that led to the car accident did. Remember what I told you?"

"Yes."

"Don't let people change your mind when you already know the truth—even when they're using 'God' to convince you. You have to know for yourself. Did the people in the store know me?"

"No."

"Then why let them get under our skin about something they don't know?"

"I didn't like it when the boys stared at you."

"People stare all the time, Zoë. It doesn't bother me one bit."

She hesitated, and then said, "But I'm not there with you when it happens."

The lightbulb came on for me. When I'd asked who she felt bad for following the incident, it was not completely true when she said it was me. It made her feel sorry for herself too. I never made Zoë feel guilty for being embarrassed by me. Her response was normal for a girl her age. It had taken me years to outgrow my own shame, and I couldn't expect her process to be any different.

I imagined it would be hard enough for Zoë to adjust to her new life without the gawks, or being teased, because of the deformed, white woman in the wheelchair. I wanted to protect her from experiencing more undeserved adversity. So, for two years, I wasn't seen outside our home with Zoë. I would run errands and attend appointments while she was in school; and if she had an appointment, I arranged for a trusted friend to take her for me.

When Zoë was thirteen, Daloris finally came to visit. She couldn't have been here for more than an hour. Although, when she arrived, she told us that the sole purpose of her visit to Miami was to see her sister.

Daloris was polite—in my presence anyway. When I

opened the front door, she looked down at me in the chair and asked if Zoë was at home. I introduced myself, and invited her in. Zoë had been in her bedroom listening to music on an old record player she had found in the shed behind the house, so she didn't hear when I called for her to come out.

I entered her bedroom. "Zoë."

"Yes?" she responded.

"Someone is here to see you," I said with a smile, and immediately Zoë knew who had come to visit.

She nearly jumped over my chair into the hallway and ran into the living room. Zoë's smile stretched from ear to ear, exposing the metal that encaged her teeth. Daloris' arms were wrapped around her sister, but there was nothing there—no joy, or any interest at all.

"Deeeee!" Zoë said excitedly.

"What you doing, girl?" Daloris asked casually, as if it were just another day.

"I was listening to some old records Ms. Gayle let me bring in from the storage. You wanna hear it?"

"Okay."

Zoë walked Daloris back to her bedroom, and the girls were alone together for about twenty minutes. I could hear various instruments, the sounds of jazz, coming from the room. Occasionally, it would stop, and I could hear their voices again.

I poured two glasses of punch in the kitchen, and then placed them on a tray in my lap to drop off to the girls. Closer to Zoë's bedroom, I could clearly hear their conversation.

"Look at you, Z. Where you get these titties from?" I heard Daloris say.

"I just woke up one day and needed a bra," Zoë chuckled as she responded.

"Or two!" The girls laughed.

"Stop! They're not that big. The bras Ms. Gayle bought me fit really good."

"Mm hm. She treat you good though?" Daloris asked.

"Yeah. She's nice," Zoë responded.

I stalled, and eavesdropped a little longer.

"I can tell. Look at all this shit you got in here. I never had a computer when I was your age—especially not one in my own room. Damn. I didn't have my own room until I was grown."

Zoë was silent. I assumed she was torn between being grateful for the life she had, and being saddened by the fact that her sister didn't have it too.

"Where she get the money to pay for all this shit? She must

be gettin' a check—more than the check she gets for you being here too. And I know ain't no man fuckin' that."

"She good people, D. She gets me clothes and shoes, and stuff I need for school. She's nice."

"She still a damn beast." Daloris laughed.

"Don't say that about her."

"What? You got a new mama now? Your mama dead, girl."

"She treats me better than mama did. At least she talks to me."

Daloris grew quiet. "I gotta go in a minute," she said.

"But you just walked in, D. I thought you wanted to hear the rest of this record."

"What is that anyway? When did you start listening to this kind of music?"

"I don't know. I like jazz. I can paint the music with different colors, or visuals, and my own lyrics when I listen to it."

Daloris laughed, "Very poetic, lil' sis. This some white people shit."

They were both silent.

"Like I said, I gotta go," Daloris reminded her.

"I thought you came to see me."

"I am. We see each other. I can't be here all day. I gotta catch my ride back."

I went into the room and placed the cold glasses of punch on Zoë's dresser. "I brought you something to drink," I said.

Zoë's countenance pleaded with Daloris' stubborn posture.

"Thank you," Daloris said.

"She said she's about to go, Ms. Gayle," Zoë said, and crossed her arms in protest.

"Well, if she has to go Zoë, she has to go."

Daloris walked over and gulped down the punch. "I'll come back soon," she said. "It's no big deal." She put the empty glass back on the dresser. "You gonna hug me before I go?"

Zoë haggardly walked over to her sister and hugged her tightly. Her lips parted, and she exhaled deeply—a breathing exercise that had become one of Zoë's habits. It was always noticeable when she did it, but it was never done to draw attention to herself. Deep breaths helped her avoid being overwhelmed with emotions.

"I'll be back," Daloris said.

It was a lie. I saw her to the front door, and she never came back again.

~

In what ways, if any, do you think Zoë was impacted by her sister's absence?

She suffered the same loss she experienced with her mother and father, but I think the pain of losing Daloris was more difficult for Zoë to manage. Unlike their parents, Daloris was alive, and free, but had *decided* to keep her distance. I couldn't begin to explain to Zoë why such a rift existed between them—-especially after all they'd been through together. And I believe Zoë searched for those answers herself.

Do you believe she ever found any?

No, I don't. She made peace with it as much as she could. I would go as far as to say Zoë remained hopeful. Something within her trusted Daloris would come around. From my understanding, she never did.

Did Zoë form bonds with other people? Was it easy for her to make new friends over the years?

I don't know how easy it was. She was pretty, but not popular. As she matured, Zoë would challenge herself to a nonconformist instead of blending in with other kids. She went unnoticed for the most part. If she wasn't at football games, basketball games, or ditch parties, it didn't matter how cute she was because no one could get close enough to know what she was like beyond the classroom. She would mention a friend or two from school, but none who were inseparable like many teenage friendships. I started to believe Zoë preferred being alone.

As Zoë's foster mother, what would you say was your greatest contribution to her life?

She had endured a lot at such a young age. I taught her to focus, and to be fully present, in order to heal and erase the past.

Zoë was never violated physically, but to see her mother get stabbed in the chest by her father, and to experience poverty, which forced her sister into prostitution, her life's trajectory didn't seem promising. My intent was to program Zoë for peace, protection, and prosperity. I taught her to focus her thoughts and energy, to be fully present, free, and to sense the abundance that surrounded her. I told her she could have anything she desired if she focused properly, and she learned to be grateful for the simplest of things.

So, you brainwashed her?

No—the total opposite. I never desired to control Zoë, and my heart was to ensure nothing, and no one, else could—past or future. I showed her who she truly was, and I loved every speck of her truth.

~

Zoë was fifteen, and a high school sophomore. She was incredibly smart, and really enjoyed reading and writing, but struggled in math. She consistently made honor roll and, due to her level of maturity, was recognized as a leader amongst her graduating class. I saw enormous potential in her.

One afternoon, I had returned home from an appointment, and was dropped off at the front door by public transportation. Zoë owned a bicycle, and would ride it to nearby convenience stores, or to a private lake a few blocks away. She would chain it to the wheelchair ramp at the front of the house when rainy weather didn't threaten to rust the bicycle's chains; but her bicycle wasn't there, and it started to drizzle. I was certain she would get caught in the rain and return home soaked.

I went into my bedroom, and listened for her arrival. There was nothing for a while. The house was quiet. In the kitchen, I pulled out a few ingredients to make a sandwich. As I turned from the fridge, I glanced from the window and noticed the shed door slightly swing open and closed. It had been left unlatched. I placed the container of sliced bread on the counter, and went towards the back door. The shed would have to be closed completely before the rain could ruin what was inside.

I opened the heavy, wooden door and noticed Zoë's bicycle lying against the ground, and knew she was in there. It would be easier for her to close and lock it when she came out than for me to take the ramp out into the rain myself. Zoë's name was on the edge of my lips when the door suddenly opened wider, and a boy stepped out. Rain slapped against his face as he buttoned his pants. I watched in amazement. He quickly shuffled around the house, and was gone.

Zoë emerged from the shed a minute later, hair disheveled, and wearing a light-green sundress. She immediately walked towards her bicycle and lifted it from the ground. When she looked up, she noticed me. She paused a second as we locked eyes, and then walked her bicycle around the house.

I heard her come through the front door as I continued to prep my sandwich.

"When you get back?" Zoë asked when she entered the kitchen. Her hair had gotten wet, and she smoothed some of the loose strands up into her ponytail.

"A little while ago," I responded, and slathered mustard over a slice of bread.

"Did it go well?"

"What?"

"Your appointment."

"Yes."

We tried to avoid the conversation we both knew was inevitable.

"You want to tell me what you were doing in the shed?"

She didn't say anything. She folded her arms and stared at the floor.

"I saw him. Does he go to your school?" I asked.

She nodded.

"What were you doing in there?"

She kept her silence.

"Are you having sex, Zoë?"

She looked over to me with droopy eyes.

"It's okay. Just tell me."

"Yes," she said shamefully.

I already knew the answer, but was not prepared for her to say it. "Okay," was all I released.

"Do I have to leave?" she asked.

"What? Leave? And go where?" I responded.

She still awaited the answer to her question.

"No, Zoë. Why would I make you leave?"

"It's wrong," she said shyly. "I shouldn't have done it."

"Is that how you really feel? Or is that what you think I want to hear?"

She contemplated my question.

"Can I ask you something?" I said, and she nodded. "Why did you?"

"Did I what?"

"Have sex with *that* boy? Why him?"

Zoë shrugged.

"Did you feel pressured into having sex?"

"No."

"Did he tell you he wanted to?"

"Yes, but I'm the one who said to meet me here."

"Do you know *why* you did that, Zoë?"

"I wanted to, I guess." She rolled her eyes up towards the ceiling, and breathed deeply. "That sounds so bad."

"Does it sound bad to you? Or do you think it sounds bad to me? Regardless, Zoë, it's okay if it's the truth. My biggest concern is that you don't know why you're doing it."

She leaned against the kitchen counter as she became comfortable in her conversation with me.

"It wasn't my first time, Ms. Gayle," she confessed. "It feels good to be with a boy like that."

"Do you do it for his attention? To make yourself more available than other girls?"

"No. I don't want attention."

"Then what do you want?"

Zoë stared at the floor again. She couldn't describe the desire for sex rooted deep within her, but she acknowledged it was there. She wanted to say something to make me not perceive her exactly as she was—a girl too young to fully understand the ramifications of sex.

"Sometimes we can't describe why we're wired the way we are. There could be a number of reasons you've chosen to have sex.

It's not my place to diagnose you. I can't." I placed a few turkey slices on top of the bread. "I want you to be healthy—mind, body, spirit."

"I feel fine," she insisted with a smile.

"Will you do it again?"

She was shocked by the audacity of my question. Her eyes rolled towards the ceiling again, "I don't know, Ms. Gayle."

"Okay. Do me this one favor: before you do it again, take a moment to think about why you want to do it. What part of you does it satisfy?"

"Okay."

"And I want you to take something for birth control too."

"Okay."

"I'll make the appointment for you."

She turned to exit the kitchen.

"I'm not judging you, Zoë; but as you go through this life, do not allow someone else to tell you what you're worth. They'll always sell you short. It may take time—you being so young—but one day you must determine your own value. When you see yourself as bricks of gold, others can only treat you like a sack of pennies if you let them."

~

Did Zoë have sex again after that?

Does a parent ever know? I don't think any parent could know if, or how often, their child is having sex. I know she tried the birth control pill—at least two different ones—and they made her sick. I stopped picking up her prescriptions after a few months, and she didn't ask for any alternatives. I assumed she just wasn't active anymore.

It appears you condoned that behavior. Teenagers shouldn't be having sex.

You're right. I accepted a behavior I did not understand. Just because I don't understand something, doesn't mean I have to

183

express my naïveté with anger and punishment. I didn't want Zoë to engage in behaviors she didn't fully understand no matter what they were––sex, drugs, bad relationships, friendships, after school activities. I weighed them all the same. I wanted Zoë to understand good decision-making, and not only when it involved what society deemed as "wrong" or detrimental to her health, or the ones with which I did not agree or understand. She determined for herself what was good for her, or bad for her, based on how it made her feel. It was her only measuring stick.

She wasn't like the girls we see depicted in films and books. She never came home with heartbreak drama, or cried her eyes out over some boy who didn't treat her right. I cannot recall a single incident where a boy was the cause of any negative emotions, or pain. It's possible she continued to have sex; and if she was, it didn't distract her or cause her to move out of her normal element. I watched for signs of that, and they never came.

But you permitted her to get to that point.

I don't expend energy on situations beyond my control. Did your parents have control over the first time you experimented with sex? Your first kiss? The first time you allowed a boy to touch you in places you knew should be off-limits? How old were you? Do they know the day you lost your virginity? Or the times you decided to skip class, or hang out with someone they didn't approve of, or take something that wasn't yours? Or, do they know of the times you lied to get out of an assignment or to take a day from work?

```
Only locking Zoë in her room could ensure
she wouldn't participate in risky behaviors,
but doing so would help neither of us. She
was free to learn some tough lessons--some
she may have never shared with me. She took
ownership of her body, and I was proud of
her. She was blossoming into an amazing young
woman.
```

~

When Zoë was sixteen, I believed the turnaround I observed in her life could be duplicated in another child. Zoë was extremely busy her junior year of high school. I had bought her a used car. She drove herself back and forth to school, and could participate in activities without depending on a bus that would drop her off as late as 8 p.m. on school nights. She had her independence, and I trusted her with it, but I didn't see her as much as I had in previous years. It was only a matter of time before she would be gone. So, I welcomed a second foster child. She was the same age Zoë was when she had come to live with me, but not as sweet. I must have sent out a vibration that summonsed a child with even deeper issues than Zoë's, and I got my wish.

Her name was Chrystal, and I was her fourth foster parent that year. She had been taken from a home where her mother, and her mother's boyfriend, sold and used crack cocaine. At our first encounter, she was quiet and a bit timid—just as Zoë had been. What made Chrystal's transition different, was that I had Zoë's help. Zoë knew what it was like to be in a new place without old faces, and she would help comfort Chrystal, play an occasional game with her, and help her with various things around the house.

On her third night with us, something bizarre happened. We all went to bed before 10 that evening. After 1 a.m., I was awakened by screams from Chrystal's room. I quickly went to see what was wrong. Zoë was already outside her room, watching the girl as she screamed in her sleep.

"I don't want to go in there," Zoë said to me.

"I have to see what's wrong."

I passed through the doorway, flipped the light switch, and moved closer to the girl in the bed. She screamed again—mouth gaped open and eyes tightly shut.

"Chrystal." I nudged her, and she made a gurgling noise. "Chrystal."

She opened her eyes and sat up quickly. She breathed heavily.

"What's the matter?" I asked her.

"What?" she said.

"You were screaming."

"You woke us up," Zoë said from the doorway.

"I wasn't screaming," the girl said.

It was definitely strange, but there was nothing more to say.

"Okay. I just wanted to make sure you were okay."

"I'm okay," she said, and nestled beneath the covers.

"Let's go back to bed, Zoë. She's fine."

"That shit is not fine," I heard Zoë say to herself as she walked into her bedroom.

The following day, I wanted to discuss the events of the previous evening. Again, Chrystal had no recollection. Her nighttime behavior was consistent. Each night, between 1 and 2 a.m., we were tortured by her screams. Some nights, they didn't last long; on some others, Zoë and I would meet at her door and wake her from her fits. Zoë had grown exhausted, and so had I, but I was still hopeful.

After a week, I had received the transfer documents, and was ready to enroll Chrystal in a nearby school. She suffered from dyslexia, and had fallen behind a grade level, so was only in fifth grade.

I was at the dining room table with Zoë one evening. We were reviewing one of her essays when Chrystal walked in.

"You ready for tomorrow?" I asked her.

"For what?"

"You're going to school," Zoë said.

"I don't wanna go to school."

"You don't have much of a choice. I have to enroll you in school."

"I won't go."

"You have to go to school," Zoë said. "It'll be alright. You'll have a new teacher, and might even make some new friends."

"No. I just wanna go back to my mama."

"You can't do that right now," I said to her.

"Well, I'm not going to school."

I placed Zoë's essay on the table and pushed back in my chair. "I understand it can be hard. I can help with your reading if that will—."

"I'm not going!" she yelled and stormed off to her room.

"Good luck tomorrow," Zoë said jokingly, and we continued with her essay.

I needed all the luck I could get. I was fully dressed when I went into Chrystal's room the following morning—ready to enroll her in school. She was still asleep. Zoë was already prepared to head out for the school day, and had grabbed a bowl of cereal from the kitchen.

"Chrystal. It's time to get dressed for school." She rolled over. "Come on. Get up," I said.

"I'm not going."

"Yes, you are."

"You not gonna make me," she said when she sat up in bed.

She was right. I had no physical ability to make her do anything.

"Zoë!" I called, and she came into the hallway with a bowl of cereal in her hands.

"I'm trying to get her dressed," I told her.

Zoë stepped into the doorway. She said, "I put your clothes over there, Chrystal. Put them on so you can go to school."

"I'm not going to school."

Zoë didn't argue. She thought of the thing the child possibly feared most, and used it to get her to comply—sending her elsewhere.

"I guess Ms. Gayle should just call the social worker and get you placed somewhere else."

"I don't want to go!"

"Then get dressed and go to school," Zoë said.

"No!"

Chrystal charged towards Zoë, who swiftly moved out of the way, and her body rammed into the side of my chair. As it fell over, I hit my head against the wall leading to the hallway, but was still conscious. I could see Chrystal attempt to massage the pain out of her side and abdomen. Zoë placed her nearly-empty bowl on the floor and came to my aid.

"What the hell you do that for?" Zoë asked.

"She can stay down there for all I care. I said I won't go to school."

Zoë helped me into the chair. I had a small scrape on my forehead where tiny specks of blood had come to the surface.

"That's what you get," the girl taunted.

Once I was securely back in my chair, Zoë rushed over to Chrystal and grabbed the collar of gown. She shoved her towards the dining room and whispered into her ear. Immediately, the girl settled, and she sat there for two hours until CPS arrived.

Zoë missed school to ensure the situation at home was

taken care of, and that Chrystal didn't cause any more harm. I was distraught, and retired to my room for the day. Zoë would check on me every hour to see if I was okay, if I had developed any new pains caused by the fall, or if I wanted to eat. She was genuinely caring and concerned. And, although I asked, Zoë wouldn't reveal what she whispered to Chrystal to get her to sit still and be quiet.

It would be a great ego-stroke to foster parent *and* help transform children's lives, but that incident caused me to drop the ego. I learned to be satisfied with just one. Zoë was enough.

About a week after Chrystal was taken away, I wrote a heartfelt letter to Zoë. By then, I knew how deeply Zoë loved me, and I asked if she would allow me to adopt her. A day later, she agreed in her own handwritten response. I have the letter to this day, but it's become difficult to read.

It wasn't my intent to change the dynamics of our relationship once the adoption was final, so we didn't—not her name, or my own. I was her mother, but I was comfortable with "Ms. Gayle", which she'd called me since she was eleven years old. I wanted her to remain in a groove of consistency, which felt good to us both. And I never wanted to be without her—my daughter, Zoë.

~

Did you believe Zoë would kill herself?

No, but it happened. She took her baby out into the garage and cranked up her car. Zoë knew the dangers of doing that. She was 16 when I bought her that car. There's only a small, one-car garage attached to this house, so of course it was her spot since I'm not able to drive. She would come home from school, pull in, sit there and listen for a song to end. I remember going to the door, flashing the lights, and yelling for her to turn off the engine while she was parked in there. I may have corrected her twice, and I didn't see her do it again.

Zoë was found with oxycodone in her system. She didn't drink or use drugs.

Yes. They told me.

Did you ever consider that someone could have made this look like a suicide?

There was no indication anything of the sort happened.

There are quite a few inconsistencies based on an interview I conducted with the responding officer. You were the only one who could have received all the details of her death. Did you even look into it?

No. I accepted what happened to her. What would it benefit anyone to do anything other than that? Accidental or intentional, she's gone.

Wow. I'm sure if Zoë were a young, white woman, police would have dug a little deeper. You call Zoë your daughter, but the death of a girl who was biologically yours, wouldn't have been so swiftly swept under the rug.

I don't understand where you're going with this.

I'm sorry. I've distracted from the point of this interview.

No. I would like to hear what you meant, so I can understand the cause of that statement.

People like me are constantly on the short end of justice. I just think there is more to Zoë's death, if anyone bothered to look.

189

Perhaps it's what you *want* to see. "People like you" will only see injustice if all they expect is injustice.

No one expects that.

Not true. No one *says* it, but most expect it. I can say I want something, regardless of what it is, but I won't receive it if my mind constantly rehearses the possibility of not having it––or if I keep reflecting on those before me who didn't get it for themselves either.

Did you teach Zoë to turn a blind eye to injustice too, especially those involving black people?

No, I taught her to focus more on what she *could* do than on what she couldn't. She had become aware of our interconnectedness––not just being black––and knew she was a key component in the functions of humanity.

If I tell you we are one, you wouldn't accept it. You could name ten differences between you and I without taking a second breath. We all come from Source, the Creator, God, but many focus more on what we don't have in common than our most unifying truth.

Even with your handicap and your deformities, you can still rest easy when you're not concerned about getting shot on the street, or in your car, or in your home as you enjoy a bowl of ice cream.

You choose to be afraid––to worry.

Who would choose that? Why wouldn't it create concern in our community? Are you implying that I shouldn't be concerned for the safety of my people?

You are not concerned for *all* black people—just the ones who are killed by under-trained, black-fearing officers, and bigots with hate deeply rooted in their bones.

That's not true.

Then who killed Zoë Sapp? She's black—-and you assume someone killed her. So, who?

You've done your homework. Why are you not outraged by the number of kids lost to gang violence each year, or blacks who've tried and can't rise out of impoverished communities, or wage and employment disparities? These are all injustices faced by the same people.

That's typical of someone like you. Deflect to an issue that—-.

That you are not able to change—-at least not from your position, and not alone.

So, I should do nothing then.

No, that's not it either. You are at liberty to fulfill the purpose you have here on earth. And only you know what that is—-but do not impose your quest onto others whose purposes are not in alignment with yours. Do *your* part, and accept that others have their own part. That's the first step. Without it, you'll spend more energy working against each other than on achieving a goal.

White people have it all figured out, huh. So, it is not that this nation stands on the successful oppression of blacks, but that blacks can't unify enough to surpass the oppression? That's why we're being killed, overlooked, undervalued?

It doesn't matter what I say. You'll only see and hear what you've conditioned yourself to see and hear. I won't deny the construct that was created to keep a race of people inferior and broken, but I won't pretend that there aren't very real solutions that are ignored and overshadowed by anger. Love is key. And the love I refer to begins within the individual, and it radiates outward. It's not pretending to agree for the sake of peace, but becoming peace itself. No one can argue with that.

With all due respect, Ms. Oliver, you took a chance on a little black girl with a jacked-up past. It doesn't make you a hero.

I wholeheartedly agree. You're right. I'm a hero because I was courageous enough to risk rejection and failure if a little black girl with a jacked-up past didn't take a chance on me—-but she did. And it is the same risk I would have taken if the child that was dropped off at my home was white.

You and I view the world differently, and that's okay. Whether we agree that the glass is half empty or half full doesn't matter as long as we can both acknowledge that there is indeed something in the glass. Perspective has a lot more to do with what we choose to see than our circumstances.

I can't say I agree with that.

I asked who killed Zoë, and immediately you considered a single person you suspect could have caused her harm, or a number of people who could have extended themselves to help in her time of need--a friend, a lover, maybe even me. Now, I ask, how many people did Zoë's life inspire? I choose to focus on the latter. There's nothing I can do about the other. The glass is half full.

Do you have any more questions about Zoë?

Yes. Let's see. It didn't surprise you when Zoë didn't come home Christmas of 2018?

Zoë never came home for holidays. She would rant about commercialism and the pressures people faced around holiday seasons. Instead, she would surprise me with visits, which made looking forward to them more exciting.

How often would she visit?

Some semesters she managed to get down here once a month. Towards the end of her second year, she started to have car trouble and could only make it once every other month to reduce the wear on her car. I only visited Tallahassee on two occasions: her freshman move-in day, and during her stay in the hospital when Honest was born. On both occasions, I wore my prostheses, and carried a cane, but I seldom travel in my condition.

Zoë joined a discreet, battered women's group, but I don't fully understand why. Nothing indicates she was abused.

It took Zoë years to completely detach from the nightmare of her mother's death. She couldn't discuss it without tears, but around her junior year in high school, every negative emotion that resulted from the incident had been spent. When she went off to college, she attended those group meetings at least twice each month to share her mother's story with the women who decided to stay in abusive relationships. She believed it was her part. A second explanation: I think she wanted to hear why the women in those meetings decided to stay with their abusers. She desired to understand her mother's decision to stay with her father in spite of his abusive nature, but her mother wasn't around to answer.

Zoë would seldom reflect on the pain of her past, or the fears of her future. Each day's energy was depleted by actions she *could* take to move forward, and not with sorrow or regret for what she couldn't change. It may have seemed small in the grand scheme of things, but her contribution to those meetings were the small puzzle piece that helps to fill one of many voids within our society. Everyone has their part; that one was hers.

What was it like the last time you spoke to Zoë?

Zoë was supposed to come home the day they found her and Honest in the car. Around midnight, my phone rang, and I knew something was wrong because I don't typically receive calls at that hour.

~

After Zoë graduated and went off to college, I busied myself with writing, collecting various antiques, and making jewelry with healing stones to sell online. Life for me was peaceful, and had very few surprises. Zoë had a routine, and would call at least every other day. We would talk for a while about school or various activities and, after he was born, we would talk about Honest. I had never experienced childbirth, but I offered sound advice on the various stages newborn babies would experience. If nothing else, I was here to listen to her motherly discoveries and trials; and she had found a good balance.

I was never alarmed, or considered things weren't as they appeared with Zoë. She told me she had been able to save money while she worked part-time, and the extra scholarship money would keep her afloat. Zoë never asked for anything. When Honest was born, I handed her $300 in cash to help them get settled—you know, diapers and formula—and she promised to tell me if she needed more. Although I knew how stubborn Zoë could be, and how much she desired her independence, I trusted the call would come if she was ever in need. When it did, I wasn't prepared for what I would hear.

It was after midnight, and I had only fallen asleep an hour earlier. My cell phone rang on the nightstand, and I could see it was her. I couldn't get out a clear "hello" when she started to speak.

"Ms. Gayle," I heard Zoë's voice on the other end. It was soft, and full of worry.

"What's wrong, Zoë?"

"I'm fine." I could hear her shuffling around. "It's really cold in here."

"Why don't you turn up the heat?"

"The power in my apartment was cut off today."

"You didn't pay the bill, Zoë?" I asked.

"No."

"Why not?"

"I don't have the money," she admitted.

"Why didn't you tell me, Zoë? I could have given it to you."

"I know."

"It's fine. I'll pay it for you in the morning, and they should turn it back on."

"It's no point. I only have another week in this place."

195

"Where are you going?"

"I'm being evicted."

"Oh, my. Why are you telling me this now?"

"I wanted to do it on my own."

"But you have me. What about school—your classes?"

"I'm not enrolled this semester."

I sighed deeply. "Okay. Don't worry. Come home for a little while, and we'll get it all straightened out."

"Okay," she whispered.

"It's late. I don't want you on the road tonight, but at sun-up, head down here. Do you have money for gas?"

"No. And I barely have any in the tank."

"Okay. How can I get some money to you?"

"Maybe we can download CashApp or PayPal."

"What's that?"

"It's an app you can put on your phone to send people money."

"I'm over 60, darling. You know how I am with technology. Do you still have your bank account?"

"Yes."

"I can put whatever you need in your account tomorrow—first thing. I'll call when we hang up to arrange for transportation to pick me up and take me straight to your bank when they open."

"Yes, ma'am."

"Hold your head up. I can hear the disappointment in your voice. There is nothing wrong with needing help. Let me do it for you. Remember, one day at a time."

"I love you," she said.

"I love you too."

We hung up without discussing how she would get through the night in the dark, and without heat. I placed the call to request a ride to the bank the following morning, and I didn't sleep much at all that night. I wanted Zoë back at home with me. I wanted to comfort her and reassure her that everything was fine.

I struggled for some time to understand why Zoë had waited so late to confide in me. And one day, I simply let it go. Zoë was entitled to her decision to keep me in the dark. All I could do at that point was help her however I could, and I tried.

On my way to the bank the following day, I called her repeatedly. I needed to know how much she wanted me to deposit. The driver waited a half hour before insisting he had other patrons to pick up for their appointments, so I went inside and added $500 to her account. I called her again during the ride back home.

Something wasn't right, but I waited to hear from her.

It was almost 5 o'clock that evening when I heard a knock on the front door. Zoë had received the money and made her way home—so I thought. Instead, a uniformed police officer and a woman in plain clothes stood outside my door. They were sent to deliver news that Zoë would not be coming home to me.

~

Zoë experienced a lot throughout her life, and had successes that others with her history don't normally have. What would you say was Zoë's greatest achievement?

Her survival. Her determination to express herself freely. Nothing else mattered to her, so it didn't matter much to me either. It didn't take a monumental occurrence or accomplishment for Zoë to celebrate herself.

Ironically, her greatest reward was knowing she didn't need a reward to be happy or express who she really was. She didn't seek anyone's validation. For me, getting out of bed, into my wheelchair, and washing up at the bathroom sink doesn't come with certificates or applause; but those are my daily achievements. Zoë learned to be grateful for the things that would go unnoticed by most people. And when the major accolades came, there wasn't any heightened excitement on her part. Others were merely recognizing what she had known about herself all along.

Was there a time when Zoë failed at something?

What we felt about accomplishments, we felt about failures. If there were moments along her path that others consider "failures", we didn't acknowledge it in that way. Every moment is a stepping stone to the next. We lived a state of acceptance, and allowed ourselves to move on--not bask in defeat, uncertainty, disappointment, and dwindling self-esteem. Zoë understood her options, and she never chose to keep herself in bondage.

What would Zoë have wanted to be remembered for?

That can only be answered by asking those who knew her what they remember most about her, or how her presence made them feel. She lived with intention, and she was satisfied with making her mark in very subtle ways.

May I see her room?

These are all the things Zoë left behind when she went off to college. She loved higher consciousness books--Dyer, Tolle, Hicks, Scovel Shinn, Murphy--and they're all over those shelves over there.

There is a bin of her old high school notebooks and journals near the closet. You're welcomed to take some of them. There's no sense in hoarding her things. I just haven't gotten around to repurposing this room.

Thank you. I should be heading out. I'll return these to you when I've completed the article.

No need. I want you to understand something. No one dies before they give up. No matter the circumstances, a person chooses to fight to live. The ones who die, are those who have given up. Zoë understood what it meant to live—-even after everything she'd gone through. I only wonder what caused her to give up when she did.

I think there is an element more powerful than our pasts engrained in the world we live in, and we're oblivious to it. What is this force that brings strong, resilient, tenderhearted individuals like Zoë to their knees? I think the question should be explored as you continue your research.

CHRISTINE RACHEAL

FINAL NOTES

Date: Sunday, January 19, 2020
Time: 8:08 PM
Location: Tallahassee, Florida

The excitement and anticipation of each interview kept me awake at night, and by Sunday, I had probably accumulated only 20 hours of sleep for the week. To say that my energy had been fully depleted is an understatement. I longed for the comforts of my own apartment and soft, queen-sized bed, but on the road back to Atlanta, I was moved by some invisible force to return to Tallahassee instead. My trip would be prolonged.

There wasn't any groundbreaking information or new evidence there for me, but I visited a few of the places Zoë frequented during her time there. I went to the all-night coffee shop where Travis' plans caused her life to change course; the café that hosted a live band three nights a week, and where she could be found dancing alone; the canopy road a few miles from campus that she travelled on bike with Destiny; the bakery where she purchased a single cupcake each birthday; and then I went to Lake Bradford.

I am a complete novice, but I managed to row the canoe into the middle of the lake. I intended to capture what it was like for Zoë in that quiet space. There was only a single vessel in sight, and I'm sure the chill in the air kept others at bay. I placed my paddle inside the canoe as it neared sunset, and then laid back to stare up at the sky.

As I slowly drifted away from my stopping point, my first thought was: Even if there was cause for Zoë to take her own life, taking the life of her newborn son would make her a murderer. Nothing mentioned in my interviews with those closest to her pointed to the idea that she would commit such a heinous act. Second: Would the record ever be changed to show an accurate cause of death—-that she wasn't a woman so tormented that she would give up on life? Or would she forever live in infamy as the college senior who killed her kid in the front seat of an old car?

Then, I pondered: Without Zoë, how else could Marcus have learned to put the pleasure of someone's genuine presence above the shallow needs of his penis? Or who could have better embraced a deformed woman by giving her lifelong anguish meaning and purpose? Or loved a friend through her recklessness? And visions of Zoë dancing alone to live jazz musicians, reciting poetry to young people in the detention center, and holding back her best friend's hair as she vomited in the dorm's showers, appeared so vividly.

Zoë Sapp was a vibrant, loving individual who arose from the ashes of her past, but a little soot had been trapped in her lungs. Not even her adopted mother's wisdom and spiritual practices could reach the crevices of Zoë's brokenness, but she was the epitome of what it means to be a survivor. So, why is she gone?

Gayle mentioned that "no one dies before they give up." I thought of the millions of men and women who have perished from illness and disease, and those who fully recovered from the *same* illnesses and diseases. I thought of those who were shot or stabbed to death, and those who suffered the same injuries and managed to escape with their lives. Perhaps Gayle was on to something. The difference between those who lived, and those who died, was a severe unwillingness to give up. If what Gayle spoke is true, I wondered what caused Zoë to give up after everything she had already worked to overcome. Was it the baby? The pressure of feeling like she had to do everything alone? The friend who used her as a scapegoat for her own deep-seated dysfunctions? Or the resentful sister who failed to reciprocate her affections? Could it be all of these things, or none at all? It was hard to decipher what mattered most, and least.

Instead of consistently revisiting what could have caused Zoë to quit, I shifted, and focused my thoughts on what, or who, had caused Zoë to live. There was nothing more than the baby she had birthed only three months prior to her death; and, ironically, she had taken him with her. This awareness raised a new level of questions: What future could Honest have had? Why was his life cut short? How could he also "give up" before fully knowing what it entailed?

After my heightened emotions for a baby I had never met settled, I realized that very few people ever met Honest—only Zoë's neighbor, who was blessed by his presence, and her adopted mother, who avoids unhealthy attachments to others. Perhaps the child wasn't meant to be in this earthly dimension longer than he had been. Perhaps he was an angel, sent to bring his mother to a place where she would have total peace and immunity from suffering. I tossed these ideas around in my head for at least an hour before I settled on the fact that, as disheartening as losing someone so incredibly innocent is, none of that mattered either.

When I sorted through old notebooks filled with poetry and essays written by Zoë in high school, I came across a reflection on Kate Chopin. Chopin was an American feminist author whose stories often depict the tragic end of women's lives. I was very familiar with the works of Kate Chopin, but most of her narratives had eluded me. I remembered the story of the woman in *The Awakening*—she'd killed herself. There was "The Story of an Hour" where the female protagonist dropped dead of heart failure after the joy of her husband's death was quenched by the fact that he was still alive. And then there was the story of Desiree in "Desiree's Baby" who killed herself by walking into a marsh with her baby in tow. And there—in Zoë's own words—was a brief reflection:

Although black women are statistically the last to successfully commit suicide, the thought and possible excitement of life on the other side of a troublesome world has crossed many of their minds. It is understandable for a woman to end her life when she can no longer be the light she needs to illuminate her own path in such darkness. We frown upon her decision to rejoin nonphysical when she can no longer create her own peace on earth...

I was initially appalled by Zoë's reflection, especially because it was being expressed by someone her age; but I've come to understand that it was the type of person she was. I won't adopt the cliché of her being "wise beyond her years", but I will say she adopted mechanisms that yielded mature decision-making, made her accepting of others, and that completely isolated her from the "normal" thinkers of the world. While the bliss of total harmony was desirable, and sought after, could it have led to an unexpected pit of loneliness as the pool of people who could truly understand her became increasingly small? Was blending into the world impossible, but loneliness unbearable? Was she trapped between the two?

Furthermore, the issue with being "strong" and "resilient" is that others forget that strong, resilient people are also human. Sometimes strength is derived from the love one receives when they're weak and vulnerable. Is it possible that Zoë failed to receive what she needed in those final hours?

If some say Zoë intentionally took her life, and that of her newborn, her history of trauma and rejection would support their claim. If others believe her death was purely a tragic accident, her consistently carefree nature, and the love she had for Honest, would support them as well. And for those who may suspect foul-play: given the evidence, there indeed appears to be a missing piece. Perhaps it doesn't matter what we believe. Zoë's gone. That's the one truth we can all rest on. But a second truth, and I'm sure some may call it mere belief, is that her death was completely preventable. Through this experience, I learned that a community must first love and protect each other. If done right, it releases the need

205

and expectation to receive love and protection from beyond it.

Who could have saved Zoë from her untimely fate? We may never know the answer, but again, "everyone has their part".

An Untitled Goodbye

Emojis presented smiles never created with my face.
I'd practiced a "Good" response to "How are you?" each
morning I'd awake.
No one saw beyond the beauty of my glowing skin.
No one saw the ugly, the deeply buried pain within.
I wanted to be better, attempt a life a normalcy,
But there was no way to escape the person that was simply
me.
I would have asked for different if I had the chance.
I didn't deal the cards, I barely played the hand.
This one was losing, but I gave it all I had.
It seemed I could never win, and life was filled with dread.
Peace be unto you, wherever you may be.
I pray that life is plentiful and, above all, that you are free.
Please don't shed a single tear at the thought of this.
In peace, I'm resting finally, but it's you that I will miss.
I love you.

```
Written September 7, 2018
by the author of this book
              (She lives.)
```

There is help.

Call the National Suicide Prevention Lifeline
1-800-273-8255

ABOUT THE AUTHOR

Christine Racheal (Ray-shell) has authored several novels and nonfiction works, and is the founding owner of Airris Books, a self-publishing consulting firm. She resides in the Atlanta area with her husband, Larry, and their children.

To learn more, and to order additional titles by Christine Racheal, visit:

www.CHRISTINERACHEAL.com

and

www.AIRRISBOOKS.com

www.ingramcontent.com/pod-product-compliance
Lightning Source LLC
Chambersburg PA
CBHW020112180626
46812CB00006B/2564